Romanced by the Rat

A Ghostlight Falls Story

G.M. Fairy

Artwork by Mairena J.

Cover Design by Unfortunate Design

First Edition 2025

ISBNs: 979-8-9996915-0-7 (paperback), 979-8-9914470-9-6 (ebook)

Content Warning

Romanced by the Rat is not suitable for all readers. For a full list of content warnings, please visit gmfairyauthor.com

To all the girlies who wondered what it would be like with some help from a little friend.

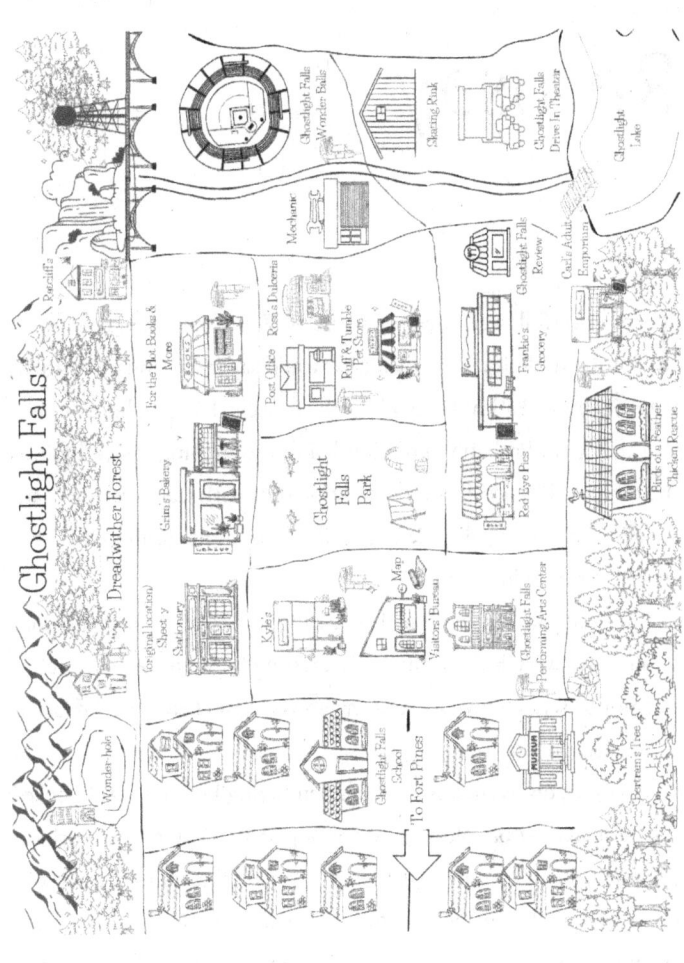
Ghostlight Falls

Chapter One

Ramsay

I'm a rule follower. Always have been. Worse than that, I volunteer for the undesirable. A therapist would say it's an innate desire to please, even when I hurt myself in the process. Except I haven't been to a therapist. Probably should, but I did something easier. I joined the military. Physical labor, deprivation of luxuries, and risking death are all much more palatable than talking about my feelings. My skin crawls just thinking about it.

No, wait, my skin is actually crawling. I'm just coming into consciousness, every inch of my body buzzing with an insistent itch. I attempt to scratch my face, but my arms are too heavy, the effects of the drugs still wearing off.

Recognition washes over me, remembering before I was knocked out. I agreed—no, volunteered to be part of a mystery science experiment. I could argue that I felt pressured. The military owns our souls after all, but when the announcement went out and the room lay quiet, I barely gave it a second before raising my hand to volunteer for the cause. The reward of luxury meals and a week of rest before the procedure made the deal even more enticing. I must have been the only person who thought that, though, because I was the only one to volunteer. There was fine print, of course. Ramblings about a transformation of body and soul, yada yada. I was too busy devouring a bowl of perfectly seasoned Bolognese to pay attention.

I groan, shaking my head and attempting to roll into a seated position. I find the momentum and rest my head in my palms. At first, I think I lost feeling in my hands, but I yank at the fibers on my face, feeling the pull.

"What the fuck?" I ask, finally opening my eyes and staring around the bright white, sterile room. Everything is huge. What kind of drugs did they give me? My brain works overtime trying to remember the details of this experiment. I was told I'd be administered a drug that would heighten my abilities in espionage. I don't know shit about biology so when they started rattling off jargon about the molecular changes, I kind of tuned things out.

Maybe this is all in my head. The room didn't grow. I didn't shrink. My face isn't hairy. This is just what it feels like to have heightened senses. Yes, that has to be it. I stand, my legs wobbly, clutching my head as I take in my reflection from the metal flooring underneath me. I scream, falling to my ass, my heart hammering in my chest. I'm not groggy anymore. All my senses sharpen, especially my sense of smell. There's no way that was my reflection.

I take another look, closing my eyes and not opening them until I fully lean over my reflection. I fight my initial reaction to scream again. Staring back at me isn't the sandy-haired, muscular man in his early thirties I'm familiar with. It's not even a man at all. Gray hair, large round ears, black beady eyes—It's a rat. I'm a fucking rat.

"No. No way." I can hear my voice, and it calms me slightly. I haven't lost myself completely, maybe I can talk myself back to reason. I've seen some scary shit in the military. I can deal with whatever the fuck is going on. I push down my feelings and take in my surroundings. I remember being in this room before I was put to sleep. Except I was in a regular, human-sized bed, not a metal, miniature, elevated platform.

I'm alone in the room. I don't doubt cameras are watching my every movement, but I can't give up the chance to get the fuck out of here. It might not be the best idea. If I ever want a chance of returning to a human, I need these people, but I never would have imagined they'd change me into a fucking rat. I need to get out of here, hide, and assess their motives. Being as small as I am doesn't give me confidence in my safety. I always knew the government did some fucked up shit behind closed doors, but this is a new level.

Rats can climb. At least I'm pretty sure. I look over the edge of the metal table, the tiled floor seeming impossibly far. I don't have very many options, though. Without thinking, I climb over the side, race down the pole, not stopping until I reach the floor. Well, that's cool. I soak in the pride of my abilities for a moment before remembering myself and darting toward a wall, climbing up the textured surface, and pushing myself through the grate of the air vent.

Just as my skinny tail disappears into the shadows, the door swings open and footsteps sound. "Where'd Ramsay go?" a man asks. I recognize him as one of the scientists who administered an IV to me.

"Fuck," another man says, another bland-faced suit.

"Why didn't we put him in a cage or something?"

"The sedation wasn't supposed to wear off for several hours. I thought we had more time."

"Well, obviously you thought wrong, idiot. What do we do now?" the man sounds panicked.

The other scoffs. "Don't get your panties in a twist. It's not a big deal. We were going to dispose of him anyway. Now we know the transformation is possible. Next round, we'll work on giving the subjects the ability to communicate, and then we'll work on a way to change them back."

This must be a nightmare. Life can't really be this fucked up. I'm frozen, hanging on their every word. There's no way to change me back. Apparently, I can't even communicate, even though I swore I heard my voice; it might have been all in my head. If I didn't wake up when I did, I'd be dead, but maybe death is a better fate than life as a rat. Even with that thought, an innate instinct to survive washes over me.

"So what? We just let him go?"

"He's a mindless animal, completely transformed. He doesn't even know he used to be human. Let him starve in the vents."

Well, that can't be true. I know myself. I remember who I was before being changed into a rat—Ramsay, a quiet, antisocial soldier who lived for his duty. Looks like that devotion led to a whole bunch of bullshit. I'm going to prove them wrong the best I can. I won't die in these vents. I won't give them the satisfaction.

I turn toward the darkness, tuning into my acute senses, ready to find my way out.

***

It takes much longer to escape from the facility than I anticipated—several days, I suspect. They've got this place sealed up tight, which makes sense since they're hiding experiments of absolute terror. By the time I push my way through an exhaust pipe and my feet—well, paws—meet the fresh grass, I'm seconds away from starvation. A beetle crawls by mere inches from me, and I don't know if it's my rat instincts or my overwhelming hunger, but I contemplate taking a bite out of it. No. I may be an animal, but I need to keep an ounce of my humanity.

My feeble humanity only lasts a few more hours. My vision blurs, I lose all reason, and when a wiggly earthworm appears in my path, I can't resist the urge to sink my teeth into the slimy pink flesh. After devouring the entire thing, a wave of shame washes over me. Sure, I'm able to reason now, but I almost wish I were back in the delirium and didn't have to live with what I have become. I've been trained to use whatever means necessary to survive, but I've never seen combat. This is as rustic as it's gotten for me, and I don't think I'm cut out for it.

I continue my journey, searching for civilization. I never ventured much into the town of Ghostlight Falls outside Fort Pines, even after being stationed here for a year, but as I pass a never-ending pit bellowing with the sound of frogs known as the Wonder Hole, I recognize the area. Except I have no sense of direction and can't make out where the town is. I keep walking, finding myself in dense woods.

After several days and nights, surviving on bugs and rainwater, I'm about to give up. What's the point anyway? I'm a rat. How could I possibly live a life worth living? But then the most delectable smells waft into my nostrils. Maybe it's a mirage, but it's so heavenly I have no choice but to follow it.

A singular building comes into view. A rushing waterfall sounds nearby. It's early morning, the sun just poking out from the tops of the surrounding trees. The structure almost looks like a beacon, a gift from above, my sanctuary. I squint to read the sign adhered above the doorway. "Ratcliff's—Fine French Dining."

My stomach rumbles. It shouldn't be too difficult to scrounge together some food in a place like this. And besides, Ratcliff's? It's almost like it's meant to be.

Chapter Two

Jeremy

"Jeremy, did you get all that?" Trisha, my aggravated trainer, asks, shooting me a look.

"Um, yeah!" I reply, a little too eagerly. She just read off Ratcliff's seasonal wine list, and I most definitely did not get that. Even if I was paying attention and not thinking about what I need to eat tonight to stay in a calorie deficit, I couldn't possibly remember the different varietals and pairings of over thirty different bottles. Memory has never been my strong suit. Physical challenges, personal goals—I'm your guy, but mental shit? Nah.

"You sure?" Trisha places her hands on her hips, eyeing me with enough judgment to send me to the fiery pits of hell. Luckily for me, I'm used to judgment. In fact, I thrive on it. It's the main reason I'm so drawn to bodybuilding—the thrill of being under a watchful eye, critiquing your most minuscule movements. It makes my cock hard. If only body   building didn't have to be so damn expensive. I made a decent enough income at the supplement store, but it's not enough to cover my entrance fees, spray tans, bathing suits, protein, and supplements. Servers make more money, so when I saw that the local French restaurant in town, Ratcliff's, was hiring, I jumped at the opportunity.

The problem is, I don't know shit about the restaurant industry, which is already evident to my sour-faced trainer. The only reason I got the job is because I lied and said I worked as a server at a country club in Florida that had recently shut down. There was no one to call as a reference, and I've always been a charmer. I just had to flash a few of my pearly whites, run a hand through my blonde curls, and my manager, Kelly, was putty in my hands. Trisha doesn't fold so easily.

"Don't worry about me, Trisha. If I get lost in the beginning, I'll just give a shout to my beautiful trainer." I wink.

She deadpans. "I don't like repeating myself."

I think the more I talk, the more she hates me. So instead of making matters worse, I just nod. "Got it."

She turns back to the floor, walking through the rows of white-lined tables, explaining how the tables are numbered. I was supposed to watch a series of online videos, and Trisha is my last barrier before I'm on my own tonight. I honestly didn't think serving would be that difficult, so I opted to scroll on my phone instead of paying attention to the information. Now, as Trisha reviews my supposed training at lightning speed, I regret my decision. I've been able to escape most of my life's fumbles, which keeps my nerves relatively in check, but I can't deny the dampness under my armpits as I watch people trickle up to the host stand.

A young blonde girl walks up to me, handing me a white slip of paper. "You're up. Table ten, party of four."

I nearly shit my pants.

"Well, looks like it's time for action." Trisha pats my back and walks past me.

"Wait, aren't you going to help me with my first table at least?"

She turns around, walking backwards. "Didn't you have a shadow shift?"

I did, two days before, with a coworker named Greg, but he was too controlling to allow me to take any of the orders. I just followed him around and helped him drop off drinks. I didn't mind. It was an easy day. Now, I wish I had made an effort to try it out on my own. "Yes, but..."

"You'll be fine! Good luck."

My heart pounds thunderously as I turn to my table—a ghost couple in their fifties with two teenage ghost children. Living in Ghostlight Falls all my life made me accustomed to the supernatural, the paranormal, and all the walks of life in between. From my travels and watching TV, I've realized the population here in our secluded community in Oregon isn't the typical demographic of most places, but I can't imagine living somewhere without the differences. It makes life more fun. Except now. Now I wish the ghost family would disappear, carry on to the afterlife, so I wouldn't have to embarrass myself. I walk up to their table, pulling at my collared shirt to release the building steam. "Hi, um. Welcome to Ratcliff's. What can I get you?"

A bald, translucent man stares up at me, scrunching his forehead. "We just sat down. Give us a minute."

"Bring us some water, dear," the woman says, shooing me away. "Right, sorry about that." I never knew if ghosts could eat or drink, maybe they just like feeling like the living, but it's not the time to ask. I spin on my heels, wanting to get out of this awkward situation. I slam into Greg, carrying a tray full of beverages. I'm on my ass, soaked. Greg recovers at the last moment, standing above me, with an empty tray in his fingertips. He shakes his head, and I scramble to get up. "Sorry about that," I say to my guests, staring wide-eyed at me.

I scurry away. My white shirt molds to my body, revealing the outlines of every one of my muscles. Normally, I'd revel in the opportunity to show off my physique, especially after noticing the beautiful dark-haired woman slipping through the entrance, but I'm too frazzled. It hasn't even been five minutes on my own and I've already fucked up. I need money for my next competition. Ratcliff's won't keep me on till next payday if I continue to screw up like this.

As I walk into the back, I run my hands through my hair, heading for the closet. I search a rack for a new apron, find one, and pull it over my wet uniform. Something scampers behind me, and I scream, stumbling out of the closet and into Trisha.

"What are you doing?" she asks, clearly annoyed.

"I think there's an animal in there," my voice an octave higher than I would prefer.

"Are you on drugs?" she asks, examining my eyes.

"What? No?"

"Are you sure? Because right now you're soaking wet and stumbling out of closets shrieking like a little girl."

I straighten myself, gathering my composure. "No, I'm not on drugs. I just... Never mind." I shake my hand, walking past her to the beverage station. I need to get waters to my tables. I can't lose this job.

Even if it's infested with rodents.

Chapter Three

Charlotte

Walking inside feels like coming home. Better than coming home since that's the exact place I'm running away from. I've always wanted to visit France, but the opportunity never arose. My parents wouldn't allow me to leave the country without them, and they had no desire to travel across the world.

I'm not an idiot. As I step into the two-story   shingled building with the word *Ratcliff's* hanging over the entrance, I'm not disillusioned enough to believe I actually stepped into a real French cafe, but the regal yet straightforward decor of the place seems like a good substitute. At least for now, when it's the only piece of Europe I'll be getting anytime soon.

"Are you meeting someone?" the young blonde hostess asks, bringing my attention away from the white lined tables and rich mahogany walls.

"Oh, no. Just a table for one."

"Name?"

"Charlotte," I reply.

The girl presses a screen in front of her and then picks up a menu. "Follow me." She turns on her heels toward the dining room.

A blond, muscular waiter grabs my attention, his eyes catching mine. He's completely soaked, revealing defined pectorals underneath his tight white button-down. My cheeks heat, and I turn back to the blonde head before me, willing my heart to slow down and focusing on making it to my table.

Sure, the guy was hot, but there are plenty of hot guys in the world. I shouldn't be so frazzled by one snagging the corner of my attention. Of course, I know the reason. I haven't been properly laid in probably like, ever.

I'm not a virgin, which kind of makes it worse. I've tasted the first layer of pleasure but haven't entirely given myself over. My parents never let me out of their sight. The only time I got intimate with a man was in brief encounters in church utility closets. A man can't take his time with me when any second someone could walk in on us and slap us with a felony.

I must admit that the desire for passion is one of the main reasons I left home. I'm twenty-one years old. I shouldn't have run away, but my parents made it clear that I either enroll in med school or they would cut me off. The threat didn't scare me like I imagined they hoped. If anything, it gave me the idea that I could actually leave. The worst they could do to me is not pay for my life. I had saved enough money from birthdays, holidays, and graduations over the years to buy myself a bus ticket and secure an apartment.

Before I left, I even found a job as an online college prep tutor. The pay isn't amazing, but it's enough to get me by. I couldn't move to New York City or Los Angeles, but I found a quaint town called Ghostlight Falls, far away from my parents and their suffocating expectations. Sure, there were articles about strange lore surrounding the town's history, but I didn't care. I started a new life that is all my own. Including eventually finding a hot guy, bringing him back to my place, and letting him fuck me into oblivion. Maybe that last bit is reserved for well down the road, but I can't help my body's wish that it would come sooner rather than later. Hopefully, a mouth-watering meal will keep my desires more manageable.

The hostess motions for me to sit at the small two-person table and places a black menu in front of me. "Your waiter will be with you shortly," she says before leaving me alone.

I scan the restaurant again, noticing the tables filled with couples or families. I'm momentarily self-conscious, but no one seems to pay me any mind. Loneliness isn't a foreign concept to me. My parents hovered over me every second of my life, but I always felt the vast emptiness in their companionship. Now, I just don't have warm bodies beside me to disguise my solitude. It's on display for the world. Surprisingly, it feels more freeing than exposing.

As I take a closer look at the people around me, I realize many of them aren't actually *people*. Bodies covered in hair, wings, green skin, hooved feet, and horns are just a few of the differences I notice between myself and my fellow restaurant guests. I shouldn't be surprised. I researched the town after all, but it still takes normy me a second to adjust. My staring gets a little heavy-handed, and the gremlin sitting alone next to me captures my gaze. I smile, scanning down the small, curated menu.

My server, Trisha, comes over quickly and takes my drink order. Her smile fades as   a bang across the room grabs her attention. I follow her gaze, catching the handsome server from before   lying on the ground with a disassembled salad sprinkled around him.

"Jesus Christ," she says under her breath, and I assume she didn't mean for me to hear. She turns back to me, her customer service mask dropping back into place. "I'm sorry about the disturbance. I'll be right back with your Pinot Noir."

"No problem." I smile, examining the blond server as Trisha walks away. His cheeks are bright red, and his wet shirt is streaked with vinegar and tomato guts. He jumps to his feet, apologizing to everyone around him while picking up bits of lettuce from his chest.

Poor guy. I wonder if I'd feel for him so deeply if he weren't so attractive, but maybe I see a bit of myself in him. I've always excelled at every task I've attempted. Maybe not at first, but not with much struggle. My parents made it known from a young age that I would be a doctor when I grew up. It didn't matter which type. I at least had that choice, but no daughter of theirs would go through life without an MD. I didn't mind the expectation. In high school, I'd always been good at science. Textbooks spoke to me, and my memory held onto facts like a vice, but during my first lab in undergrad, I discovered the truth. No textbook could prepare me for actually working on a human. I'd gone deep into my research. There had to be a medical doctor who didn't practice on patients. I even considered working with dead people in some capacity, but I quickly discovered I didn't have the stomach for that either. I could have forced myself to pursue one path. I could have made it work, but it was then that I really started to reflect on myself. Did I even want to be a doctor? No. I had no idea what *I* actually desired. I needed to run away to Ghostlight Falls to find myself.

As I look at the wet, dressing-stained server, I can't help but imagine our similarities if I had barreled through and continued to medical school. I would have floundered like a beached whale. I wonder if this guy is dealing with the same affliction, forced to do something to appease another part of himself. Or maybe I'm just trying my best to find similarities between us because I'd desperately like to fuck him, even with a stray crouton on his shoulder.

Luckily, my wine comes from my left and diverts my absurd line of reasoning. I shouldn't be so drawn to him. It must be the emptiness in my stomach making everything so intense. I sip my wine as I scan the menu. There aren't many vegetarian options, but when I spot ratatouille, I know my choice. It's always been my favorite dish. I order, and am delighted that my food comes in only fifteen minutes.

The layers of red, green, and yellow form a perfect spiral in the ceramic white dish. The rich smell of herbs wafts through my nostrils, and as I pierce the soft vegetables with my fork, my mouth is already watering. The first bite is orgasmic, and I close my eyes and audibly moan as the flavors flood my taste buds. This is the best ratatouille I've ever had. Much better than any of my brief sexual encounters.

I open my eyes, surprised to find the handsome waiter wiping a table in front of me, gaze locked on mine. My heart beats faster and slower at the same time. There's want in his eyes, no mistaking it. I gulp, my cheeks heating. His lips part, and I swear he's going to say something, but Trisha walks out behind him, calling his name, Jeremy, and stealing his attention.

I'm knocked out of my trance, hot, bothered, and fidgeting in my seat. I can't return to my meal—not yet. I need to cool off. I take a sip of my ice water as I scan the fake plants lining the rafters of the ceiling. Something scurries into the shadows, and I jump. Does Ratcliff's have rats? It should gross me out, but after that bite I just had, I'd eat here again even if the rats were the ones cooking the food.

Chapter Four

Ramsay

Surprisingly, being a rat isn't half bad. Okay, no. It fucking sucks. But if I don't think about my reality for too long and instead pretend that the gourmet food I get to enjoy every night doesn't come from the garbage can, it's like I'm on a much-needed vacation. I'm the only rat in this joint, thanks to the numerous traps in the attic and around the rafters. Most rats don't know how to avoid those death pits, leaving me the smartest animal around. I could never say the same for myself when I was a human, so I revel in the small win of my dominance in intelligence.

I've always enjoyed people-watching. Thank God, because it consumes most of my time now. I felt invisible as a human. Sure, I was good-looking, but I appeared as an extra, melting into the background. I could sit on a park bench and watch people for hours, and no one would glance my way. Now, it's even more so. It's more important to stay hidden, but my small frame and ability to blend in keep me out of the patrons' eyes in the restaurant.

There's one waiter who continuously catches my attention. His name is Jeremy and he's new. He's the type of guy who probably has never felt invisible. He's impressively tall with movie-star good looks.

I don't know if he notices it, but everyone turns his way whenever he passes by. Even me. He's my complete opposite, and I can't take my eyes off him. He's a shit waiter though. I used to serve in high school, and I knew my way around the restaurant. I probably would have stuck with it full-time if they provided me with room and board. God, does he need direction, someone to lead. The thought sends a shiver down my spine and a twitch to my tiny rat penis.

Oh, yeah. I have a rat penis now. Every man dreams of a bigger dick. Being turned into a rat is too many layers of fucked up, but having essentially a micro-penis? It's a new level of despair. Okay, proportionally, it's not that small compared to the rest of my body. I have never seen another rat penis in my life, but I imagine mine would be pretty impressive. At least that's what I tell myself because God, do I need a win.

I bet Jeremy has a big dick. Why am I thinking about his fleshy member? Well, I don't have a lot to think about as a rat. I'm without modern distractions such as television or mindlessly scrolling on my phone, so now I think of dicks, specifically the blond, curly haired waiter's.

Maybe I want to be him. Maybe I hate him. Maybe something else. But as the dark-haired beauty from the day before walks through the front door, I can tell she immediately is searching for the same man who holds my attention. Envy boils in my rat veins.

I was never good with women. I've always been shy and kept to myself. There were a few who held my attention. I always became obsessed, contemplating their thoughts, their day-to-day activities. I'd write poems, draw sketches of their features in the margins of my paperbacks, and the most devastating part of it all is that they never returned my affection. Of course, it was my fault. I never made it known, too afraid of rejection.

When the dark-haired woman walked into Ratcliff's yesterday, my heart stopped. It was like all the times I'd fallen in love before, but much more intense. Some say that love at first sight is a myth, and maybe that's true. Perhaps what I feel for the woman sitting alone at the two-person table in the middle of the restaurant isn't love, but it's intense and suffocating.

It's good she's back only a day later. She might continue this trend, and then I can endlessly absorb her beauty from afar.

Jeremy walks up to her table, takes a deep breath, and straightens his button-down. He's been assigned her table. *Shit*. He'll be her waiter, give her a horrible experience, and she'll never return. It's not like I can run down there and remedy the situation. If his god-awful service doesn't turn her away, a rodent scurrying around sure will.

I race across the rafter, sliding down the wall and hiding in a fake plant close to her table to get a better view. If this is my last time being near her, I want to get as close as possible.

"Hi, I'm Jeremy. I'll be your server this evening." His eyes sparkle, and his hands fidget around each other. Of course, he's nervous. Every table he approaches leaves a wave of anxiety wafting off him, but he's even more uneasy than usual, and from her wide pupils to the slight part of her lips, she's just as smitten as he is.

Great. She'll fall in love with him, ignore his failures, and return daily.

And I'll watch.

Somehow, this is worse than him scaring her away.

"Hi, Jeremy. I'm Charlotte."

Charlotte. The name feels like chocolate melting in my skull. I'm lost in the sensation of this new information. My recent obsession has a name. I barely register the thick silence that passes over the two until I can practically taste the tension on my tongue.

"Oh, um...Well, can I get you something to drink?"

She startles, shaking her head and regaining her train of thought. "Right, yes." She scans the menu, her eyes darting. "I'll take the house, Pinot Noir."

"Got it." He turns on his heels, but stops in his tracks and turns back to her. "That's wine, right?"

Her face scrunches in confusion before she cracks a smile, the most beautiful, diamond-breaking smile I've ever seen. She waits for him to reveal the joke.

"Sorry, I'm new," he says, scratching the back of his curly mop.

"Oh, that's okay. Yes, red wine."

"Got it!" He points finger guns at her before skipping away.

God, is this his attempt to flirt with her? Charlotte watches him, confusion skewed across her perfect face. It's almost like I can feel her arousal deflating. I doubt she's the type of woman to judge someone based on their lack of intellect, but it's like she's bringing herself down to earth, telling herself that he's just not that into her. I like to imagine that if I were him, I'd pick up on her signals better, push forward, and reveal that her feelings were reciprocated. I'm not sure if it's the truth. I've never been bold, but if I looked like Jeremy, I'd like to believe I would be. If only I could be him, control his perfect self to make my dreams become my reality.

Jeremy returns fifteen minutes later. I enjoy the time without his presence, just able to watch Charlotte as she gazes around the dining room. She's a people-watcher too. I can already tell that we have a lot in common.

"Sorry about the wait," he says, placing the glass of wine down on the white linen tablecloth. Drops of red splash around the spot. Charlotte startles. "Sorry about that," Jeremy says, leaning down to clean up with a napkin in his pocket. He moves too quickly, knocking the wine glass with his shoulder and sending its contents over the front of Charlotte's yellow dress. She squeals, staring down at her ruined outfit.

"Oh my God! I'm so sorry!" He doesn't give himself a second to think before pressing his napkin against her damp chest, attempting to soak up the mess. He freezes, his hand against her breast with only a wine-soaked napkin and her damp, thin dress separating them. Their eyes meet. The air thickens and my cock twitches. I can't tell if this is good or bad but I'm eager to see what happens next.

The moment falls away, and Jeremy pulls himself back. "I'm so sorry. I'm an idiot." He rubs his large hands down his face.

Charlotte parts her lips. "No, it's fine. I'm..."

"No. It's not fine. I'm new, and I am doing a horrible job. Your meal is on me. Let me go get another server so you can enjoy yourself for the rest of your dinner."

Charlotte reaches for him, to stop him, to tell him it's okay and that his accident doesn't make her think any less of him. I can see it in the small lines at the corners of her lips. But Jeremy is already stomping away, his cheeks red and his head hung low.

I've had confusing thoughts for Jeremy ever since he's shown up, but now I can't help but feel sorry for him. He doesn't know his potential. Charlotte would be putty in his hands if he just pulled his head out of his ass.

There's nothing I can do about my growing obsession for Charlotte. I'm a rat, and as far as I know, I'll always be one. There's no hope for the two of us, but Jeremy isn't hopeless. He can be guided.

Chapter Five

Jeremy

How has it only been a week of working at Ratcliff's? It feels more like a month in a war-torn wasteland. That might be dramatic. I'm working as a server at a four-star restaurant, not in a dystopian zombie apocalypse, but my nervous system doesn't know the difference. I thought this job would be easy money for my upcoming competitions, but clearly, I was wrong.

Whenever I get home from my shifts, I pass out in my uniform. I totally missed the deadline to sign up for the Mr. Bronze Super-Man competition in the next town over. What's the point of killing myself at a job I suck at when I don't even use the extra cash to accomplish the goals I got this job for?

It's not like the tips have been amazing. Most people give me the expected 18 percent, but some of the other servers walk away with hundreds of dollars every night. I'm not even close to that. Of course, I'm constantly spilling food and beverages on my tables, which doesn't lead to happy customers. I don't blame them. I wouldn't tip myself either. Especially after spilling the wine on that beautiful brunette last night, Charlotte. I wanted to crawl into a hole and die. And after ruining her dress, I rubbed her tit like a psycho.

I don't know what's wrong with me. I'm usually decent with the ladies. Okay, maybe that's not totally true. My good looks and physique lead to a lot of one-night stands, but once I open my mouth, it's all over. I haven't always been the sharpest tool in the shed, especially under pressure. I'm horrible at many things, but finding the most fucked up thing to say in a situation is where I shine. That's why I love bodybuilding. Everyone focuses on my oiled, carefully crafted aspects, and not the mess of thoughts behind my skull. Sometimes I wish I had a little person on my shoulder to whisper what I should do in my day-to-day. A guy can dream.

I step through the doors of Ratcliff's—another day in hell. No one looks me in the eye as I head to the back to clock in and put away my stuff. They probably all know I'm about to be fired. I'm surprised they let me last this long. I may be a shitty server, but I'm usually able to redeem myself by the end of my guest's meals. I'm a charmer, even if my words lack weight, and I'm able to get my tables not to hate me. It's not enough, though. I won't be here for long, and maybe it's for the best.

Before I make it to the swinging double doors, Claire, the hostess, taps me on my shoulder. "Jeremy, I know you just got in, but we have a one-top that requested you. Can you hurry up and take it?"

"Requested me?" I whip my attention to the front of the house, and my heart stops once I spot her. Charlotte, looking even more beautiful than the day before. I can't help my racing thoughts, hopeful that she saw through my failures and wants to give me another chance, but then my blood turns cold. If I didn't ruin my chances with her yesterday, a fresh day of fuckups sure will. I'm not myself here—not that *myself* is much better. I'll be a jittery mess and make her run away.

I push myself to the back, ignoring the commotion around me and throwing myself into the utility closet where the staff keep their belongings. I sit on the bench underneath the coat rack, hand over my heart as I focus on my breathing. "What am I going to do? I can't be her server again," I say to myself, hoping a pep talk in the quiet darkness will settle my nerves.

"How about starting with not spilling wine all over her?"

"What the fuck?" I jump to my feet, feeling against the wall for the light switch. The cramped room floods into view, and I scan. "Hello?" I call with a shaky voice, not seeing anyone in here with me.

"If you don't want to screw this up, you're going to need to calm down." The strange voice comes from up above, and I search the ceiling, wondering if there's a hidden speaker.

"Who are you?" I ask, growing annoyed that one of my coworkers is obviously spying on me.

The voice sighs. "You're wasting time. Charlotte is sitting out there waiting for you."

"Who are you?" I yell again.

It's silent for a moment.

"God."

"Oh, fuck off." Whoever it is isn't going to reveal themselves anytime soon.

I exit the closet, taking a deep breath before charging into the dining hall. Charlotte sits at the center of the large room. The lights overhead illuminate her like a spotlight from heaven. Her hands rest folded on the table, and she scans around the room until our eyes meet. She smiles. Jesus Christ, it's the most beautiful smile I've ever seen. My knees nearly give out, and then I remember I have to remove the distance between us.

"Hello, welcome to Ratcliff's. I'll be your server, Jeremy," I say as I approach her table.

Her smile fades. "I know. I was in here yesterday."

My cheeks heat. "Yes, of course, of course. I remember. Charlotte, I'm glad to see the wine came out okay," I say, pointing to her tit.

She looks down at her light pink shirt and back up at me. She studies me before saying, "I didn't wear this yesterday."

"Right, of course. I knew that. I'm sorry."

She nods. A thick, uncomfortable silence passes between us. I want it to suffocate me. I somehow find words. "I'll be back with some water." Before I can catch her response, I spring toward the back, cursing myself the whole way.

When I make it to the semi-privacy of the drink station, I let out a heavy sigh, coated with my self-loathing. "I'm a fucking idiot."

"That's a little harsh." It's the voice from earlier.

I whip around. "What the fuck?" It sounded as if it came right up to my ear. "How are you doing that?"

The voice comes from a different direction   this time. "You're worried about the wrong thing. I'm trying to help you."

"You're trying to fuck around with me." I peer behind the wall dividing the drink station from the back. It's deserted. It's only 4:30. Most servers don't clock in until 5, but I'm stuck with the shitty early shifts. I have no idea who could be doing this.

This is all too much. I need a second alone. I abandon the water and rush toward the bathroom, locking myself in a stall.

"Aren't you going to bring her a water?"

"Holy fuck!" I yell. "You've got cameras in the bathrooms?" I stand on the toilet, pushing up the ceiling tiles to search for the source of the voice. "Whoever this is, this is about to be a giant HR issue!" I stop my search, thinking for a moment. "Hey, maybe I can sue and then I won't have to work this shitty job."

"Good luck. I don't work for the restaurant."

"Then who are you?"

"I told you, God."

I squat down on the toilet, pulling my knees in. "Alright. Maybe I am losing my mind. Maybe I should call it a night and head home."

The voice grows stern, commanding. "Listen to me. Don't fuck this up. You may never get this chance again. You need to go back out there. Tell her she looks lovely tonight. Ask her if she wants Pinot Noir and the ratatouille again. You need to show your interest in her."

I pause my freak-out. Maybe this is a voice in my head, but I'm giving myself good advice. There's a connection between Charlotte and me, strong and impossible to ignore. The voice is right. If I ruin this, I'll kick myself for an eternity.

I sigh, exiting the stall and straightening myself up in the mirror. "Okay, fine. Not because I'm listening to ominous voices in the bathroom, but because I want to make this work with Charlotte."

"Whatever, dude," the voice says with a sigh before I exit the bathroom. I charge toward the drink station again, grabbing a fresh glass of water and quickly making my way back to my table. I focus on the directions given to me. "Sorry about the wait. Did I mention you look stunning tonight?"

Charlotte's brown, doe-eyes widen, and a smile curves at the corner of her lips. "Uh, no. I mean, thank you."

Holy shit. It's working. My confidence rises, and I puff out my chest in victory. "Would you like the Pinot Narwhal again?"

She giggles. "Good one." Her response catches me off guard. She's laughing, not shimmying out of her clothes and demanding I ravish her. Maybe this God has things wrong.

"Something else then?" The amusement drops off her face, reading pure confusion, as if my stupidity is an anomaly. "I'll have the Pinot Noir." To her defense, she doesn't enunciate the last word to accentuate just how much of an idiot I truly am.

"Right! I was just joking." I back up, tripping on nothing in my attempt to flee. I steady myself. "I'll be right back with your beverage." I shoot her finger guns, my face growing hot, and rush back to the stall. I've got some words for God.

"What the fuckkk," he says, the moment I step through the bathroom door.

"I did what you said!" I yell as I stomp against the tile and stare up at the ceiling.

"You do not. I did not tell you to see if she wanted a rare aquatic mammal. The least you could have done is make it seem like the mistake was on purpose. You're a white man. That's the one thing you're supposed to be good at."

"Well, obviously I'm not good at a lot of things."

"Yeah, except looking pretty."

The compliment catches me off guard, and I chuckle. "So you think I'm pretty?"

"Oh, fuck off. You know what I mean. Obviously, Charlotte finds you attractive. If I were you, I'd have her wined, dined, and splayed out in my bed in hours."

I scoff. "So what, you're like some disfigured god or something?"

He chuckles. "Do you really believe I'm God? Wow, you're more of an idiot than I thought."

"I don't know what I believe! We're in Ghostlight Falls after all. Anything in this town is possible, but I'm growing more and more convinced that I'm just losing it."

"If I showed you what I looked like, I'm pretty sure I'd send you on a one-way ticket to a mental hospital."

"Well, now I've got to know."

"Probably not a good idea."

"If anything, maybe it will make me feel better about myself. You're here to help me after all, right?"

He scoffs. "Not necessarily."

"Then why are you talking to me and telling me what I should do with Charlotte?"

Scuffling sounds behind me, and I whip toward the source, but nothing is there. "I don't know. I have nothing better to do," he replies.

I sigh. "Can you even show yourself? What are you, like a ghost or something?"

"No. I'm not a ghost."

"Then what?"

"Fine!" he yells. "I don't know how seeing me will make you any better at getting the girl, but if that's your mental barrier, here I come."

I wait.

Nothing happens.

"Well?"

"I'm right here."

I whip around the white bathroom. I'm still alone. "Where?"

"Right here!" He speaks up louder, this time making it impossible for my attention not to be drawn to his source. I stare down at my non-slip shoes. A tiny gray rat sits at my feet, staring up at me. I scream, falling backwards. I'm not afraid of rats usually, but even the most stoic man would be caught off guard if a tiny rodent popped out in front of them.

"Ha, ha, very funny!" I yell to the room, regaining my footing and pulling myself into a seated position.

"What's funny?" There's no mistaking it this time. The voice came from the rat. But no. Rats don't talk. At least, last time I checked. I freeze. "Who said that?"

The rat waves his fuzzy, pink-palmed hand. "It's me."

I scream again. A talking rat isn't the craziest thing I've seen. Moth-man dined at Ratcliff's just the other day, but in all my years of living in Ghostlight Falls, I've never been snuck up on by a talking rat. It's unnerving.

"Oh, calm down." He rolls his eyes. "I could have been a talking alligator. How much harm could I possibly cause you?"

He's an asshole, but that isn't new. I clutch my chest, stilling my panic and letting my head clear. "How do people normally react when you reveal you're a talking rat?"

He picks at his forelimb, looking nervous. "Well, this is my first time. Considering you haven't tried to stomp on me, I'm thinking it's going pretty well."

"Wait, do all rats talk?"

He laughs, surprisingly rich for such a little creature. "No. Well, at least not to me. As far as I know. I'm the only one. That's probably because I'm not really a rat. I'm a man, same as you. Not exactly the same as you. I was a soldier at Fort Pines. Got tricked into a science experiment and here I am." He waves his hands at his side as if presenting his form for the first time. There are several points in his explanation that he's leaving out, as if being turned into a rat is just a regular day in the office, but I have too many questions—the most pressing involving the dark-haired beauty waiting on me in the dining room.

I rub at my temples, charging toward the sink to splash cold water on my face.

The rat talks from behind me, scurrying closer. "I know it's not my place, but I have nothing better to do. I spend most of my time watching the patrons here at the restaurant. When Charlotte came in..." He turns away from me. "I couldn't look away. And then I saw she had an attraction to you, one that you reciprocated. You continued to fumble, and I just couldn't sit by and watch you ruin something that will never happen for me, but could be the greatest thing for you."

I study him. I've never observed a rat before, but his voice, his movements, they all seem so sincere—so desperate for a connection. If what he says is true and he really was a man turned rodent, I'd imagine life would be pretty boring. It's not too hard to imagine that he wants to help because he has nothing better to do. I feel somewhat sorry for him. It's a nicer feeling than feeling bad for myself. I sigh. "If you want to help me, I'm not going to stop you. I'm obviously not going to remember your advice, though." An idea pops into my mind and I brighten. "Why don't you come with me and whisper what I should do?"

The rat smiles. "That could work, but how could I stay hidden?"

I ponder for a moment. I think there are some hats in the closet. You could sit on my head and whisper to me hidden underneath my hat."

"Sure." He shrugs.

I bend down, offering my hand, and he climbs up. "I'm going to put you in my apron pocket, until I get the hat."

"Fine with me." He's an easy-going rat for sure. But maybe I'm a little too easy-going as well, offering a vermin a free ride after just meeting them moments before.

I gingerly place him in my apron before racing out of the bathroom and heading toward the closet. We wasted too much time getting to know each other. Charlotte is waiting.

Something about having him close makes me instantly more confident. I don't hesitate to pull out the short white chef's hat, placing the rat on my head, and covering him. I stop before I charge to the bar. "Oh yeah, what's your name?" It seems only fair; he apparently knows way too much about me.

"Ramsay," he says, making himself comfortable in my curls. I can't say I hate the feeling—the weight of him, feeling not so alone. I just fucking hope he doesn't have fleas. His voice makes its way to my ears easily. I hope no one else can hear him. "Hey! I actually can see through the hat," he says. "This just might work."

"Hide a bit in my hair," I whisper. If he can see out, there's a chance people can see in. He wiggles closer to my scalp.

The bar is empty. I guess the bartender hasn't clocked in yet. "Shit." I don't know which one is the Pinot Noir."

"Do you not know how to read?" Ramsay asks.

"I don't have time to read all the labels!" I yell back. A lone woman eyes me from the other side of the bar, clutching her purse to her shoulder as she makes her way from the bathroom to presumably her table. Right, gotta cool it with talking to myself so loudly.

"Walk toward those bottles of red!" Ramsay barks.

I swivel around, trying to find the "red" section.

"Jesus Christ! This way!" Ramsay tugs on a strand of my hair, sending my body lunging in the direction of his yank.

"What the fuck," I mutter, regaining balance from my knees.

"Did you just involuntarily move?" he asks, a laugh coating his question.

"How did you do that?"

He doesn't respond, only yanks my hair again, sending my feet closer to the shelf housing the bottles of dark red. He pulls a smaller strand. "Here, grab that one." My hand shoots out and clasps around the bottle closest to me. Sure enough, as I scan the label, it reads Pinot Noir. "Holy shit," I whisper.

"No time to stand with your fingers up your ass. Get over to Charlotte's table, now!" He pulls my hair again, sending me out from behind the bar and toward the dining room. I have no clue how he knows which strands of hair to direct which portion of my body, but he doesn't hesitate. I want to stop and detangle the semantics of this arrangement, but he's right, we don't have time. Besides, he's a talking rat. Nothing about this situation is normal.

"Sorry about the wait!" I yell once Charlotte comes into view.

"Lower your voice," Ramsay scolds. I tense wondering if she heard him. Charlotte just looks from my face to the bottle of wine in my hand without a hint of confusion coating her expression. Good.

"Oh, no problem. I was just scanning the menu. What are *Honey Holes?*"

I scratch the back of my head, careful not to knock my hat over. "It's a dessert." That's honestly all I know.

"Smooth, jackass," Ramsay whispers. Why did I agree to this arrangement again? "Pour her wine, smile, give her eye contact!" he commands.

Oh right. I needed that.

I do as I'm told. Something about having another helping hand so close sends my nerves away. My hands are steady as I uncork the bottle and pour the liquid into her glass already on the table.

Charlotte smiles at me before taking a sip. "Wow, this is great!"

"I gave her the Le Creme Rosa. It's 150   a bottle. Tell her it's your finest wine and that it's on the house."

I do as I'm told, even as my stomach tightens, because I don't know if that'll come out of my paycheck. I guess it's a good thing the bartender wasn't there to rat me out.

Her cheeks rosy. "You didn't have to do that."

Ramsay whispers more orders, and I repeat, "It's the least I can do after my mishaps yesterday. Actually, I insist on making it up to you even more. I'd love to take you out."

Her shoulders straighten. "Like a date?"

"If you'll have me," I reply, hand over my heart, just as I was told.

"Oh, um." She tucks a strand of dark hair behind her ear, and her eyes dart nervously. This was a horrible idea. What does this fucking rat know? I'm being too forward, scaring her away.

"I'd love to!" Her voice cracks slightly.

Ramsay whispers more orders. "How about tomorrow at noon? We can have a picnic at Ghostlight Falls." The town's famous waterfall stands right on the other side of Ratcliff's overlooking the water tower. It's a great suggestion on Ramsay's part—romantic, unique, secluded. My mind wanders to forbidden places, and my slacks tighten.

"That sounds wonderful." She beams, hands clasped together.

"Great! It's a date. In the meantime, I'll put in an order for ratatouille and some Honey Holes." I back up and wink before turning and walking back to the server station. "We fucking did it!" I whisper once I'm out of earshot.

"Yep," Ramsay replies. "Now you just have to not fuck it up for your date tomorrow and the rest of your life."

My heart beats faster. "Wait, no. I can't go on the date on my own. You have to come with me." I type in Charlotte's order on the POS, almost hitting the wrong button, but Ramsay pulls my finger to the correct spot.

"What are you going to do? Wear this little hat on your date?"

I think for a second. "I can wear a baseball hat. I'll cut out a hole and insert mesh so you can see!" Maybe I'm not an idiot after all.

Ramsay's silent for a moment, and I resist the urge to beg again. Having him near makes me a more confident man. Of course, this can't last forever, but I just need him until I'm comfortable around Charlotte. Then I'll be able to take the reins of this relationship.

He sighs. "Fine. It's not like I have anything better to do."

"I could kiss you right now."

"Please don't."

I laugh.

"Okay, Romeo. Let's see if I can't help you make a decent amount of money tonight." He yanks me away from the computer and to the drink station. I'd almost forgotten that I had an entire shift to work tonight. Somehow, the thought isn't as terrible as it was when I clocked in. I won't be alone. I've got a furry companion guiding me around this war zone.

Chapter Six

Ramsay

I stand outside Ratcliff's entrance, my stomach in knots. Jeremy should be here any moment, but my mind can't stop whirling with worst-case scenarios. What if he forgot to set his alarm clock? What if he gets into a car accident? He's a grown man who spent his entire life without my guidance, but after last night, I don't know how he made it so far without me.

To give him credit, he's not completely incompetent. I don't think he realizes how wound-tight he is. His nerves heighten and completely take over all of his cognitive reasoning. Thank God he decided to pursue bodybuilding instead of joining the military. He'd find some way to bomb the whole town.

We spent four more hours together last night. Not only did he secure a date with Charlotte because of me, but he also had his best night of serving yet, walking away with 300 dollars in his pocket. The guy is anything but ungrateful. He wouldn't shut up about how much easier the night was with me guiding him away from mishaps. He seemed so excited to use his money to help fund his future bodybuilding competitions. We talked about our hobbies; I with people-watching, and he with working out and letting others judge him. We're nothing alike, but we make a tolerable company.

He offered to share half of his earnings with me, saying he wouldn't even have made ten dollars without me. I declined, because what the fuck am I going to do with money as a rat? But I appreciated the gesture. I can't deny that the night benefited not only Jeremy. I crawled back to my makeshift nest in the attic above the refrigerators, feeling fulfilled and excited for a new day. I can't remember the last time I fell asleep so easily—not even as a human.

We made plans to meet at the entrance of the restaurant, where Jeremy would pick me up before his picnic date with Charlotte. I gave him a detailed list of what to pack, but I have little faith in his ability to follow it. I would have insisted on coming home with him so I could ensure the shopping and packing went smoothly, but we had just met. I didn't want to sign up to be this guy's pet yet. I enjoyed the ounce of my independence I still had.

Just as I'm about to start yanking my fur out with worry, I catch Jeremy pulling up in his beat-up Volkswagen. He swerves in the spot closest to the entrance and stumbles out, an avalanche of water bottles following him. I shake my head as he grabs the picnic basket from his trunk and walks toward me, stopping once he realizes he forgot something and turning to retrieve a baseball hat from his back seat. His face lights up after searching the ground near a   tall flower pot and catching me. "Hi! Sorry, I'm late. I couldn't figure out what to wear."

I size him up. His cream button-down, paired with tan shorts, was a good choice, except that the buttons don't line up and the hem is crooked. We don't have time for adjustments, so I remain silent as he picks me up and shows me his hat, which he stayed up late last night to cut out the black canvas in the front and replace it with a tight mesh.

From the outside, it's completely indistinguishable, and I'm surprised when he places me on his curly locks and covers me, and I can still make out the outside in front of me. I suppose the guy is skilled in arts and crafts. Who would have known?

"Where are you meeting her?" I ask as Jeremy starts toward the pebbled road leading away from the restaurant and to the crashing water in the distance.

"Near the entrance."

"Nice."

"Was that sarcastic?"

"I mean, you could have offered to pick her up, but by the state of your car, I'm guessing that wouldn't have been a good idea."

"Fuck off," he says, shaking his head.

"Oh, hi!" Charlotte calls after we walk past a bend shaded by a large tree.

Jeremy's body tenses underneath me. "Oh! Hi! Sorry, I didn't see you."

"Calm down, dip shit," I whisper, cringing at the rapid cadence of his voice. His shoulders roll back, and he takes an indistinguishable breath. He does well with direction—never fights me and calms the moment I give an order. It makes my rat dick hard, but that's probably just because it's been centuries since I've gotten laid. It's not like I'd ever consider coupling with a female rat. I'm a man, regardless of whatever fucked-up form I'm in right now. The thought turns my insides out.

Most of all, being near Charlotte has an erotic effect on me. Honestly, it's probably the main reason why I'm agreeing to this date. Even if it's just for a moment, I can pretend it's me who's charming her, making her panties wet. Well, it is actually me. God, I hope he can't feel my balls tightening against his scalp.

She smirks, brushing a strand of dark hair behind her ear. "It's okay. I just got here, so perfect timing."

An awkward beat passes, and I whisper, "Ask her to follow you. Talk about your picnic."

He clears his throat. "Well, should we head to the falls?" I pull the hair that controls his arm (no, I don't know how I know that) and have him motion toward the entrance. "I packed cheese, crackers, and some fruit. I hope that's okay?"

Good. I suspected she was a vegetarian after all the ratatouille. He listened to my advice.

"That sounds wonderful!" Charlotte beams at him, her eyes bright, brown saucers. For a second, I swear they're looking at me.

They fall into step next to each other, and I lead him closer until they're brushing arms. God, I almost feel the friction. "Ask her about how long she's lived here," I order.

"I haven't seen you around before. Are you new in town?" Nice, good spin.

"Yeah. I just moved here a week ago."

"What brought you to Ghostlight Falls?"

"It was kind of random." She appears nervous. "I knew I couldn't afford living in a big city, and I wanted to be somewhere far from home. I sort of just closed my eyes and stuck my finger on a map, and here I am."

"Running from something?" he asks.

"No! Too serious and probing. Make it lighter," I whisper through gritted teeth.

He laughs. "I'm just kidding. I get wanting a new start. I think about getting away and starting over all the time." We reach the pool at the bottom of Ghostlight Falls. The two stop, and Jeremy subconsciously begins setting up the picnic.

"Really?" she asks. "This town seems so wonderful. And Ratcliff's seems like a great place to work."

Jeremy sits on the white and red checkered blanket, folding his legs underneath him. Charlotte sits next to him. "Yeah, it's nice, I guess. I grew up here, so the quietness, Bigfoot, and aliens are all normal for me. But I haven't found my purpose yet. I'm pretty sure it's bodybuilding, but it's an expensive hobby. That's the reason I started working at Ratcliff's, but so far I just suck at my job and haven't been able to make enough money for a competition."

"Okay, trauma dumping much? Slow down. Ask her about herself," I whisper after his monologue.

"You do bodybuilding?" she asks. Great. Charlotte seems like an intellectual, someone who can sit for hours alone and just people-watch. I don't think the idea of oiled, beef cakes would be her thing. It's a practical question, though. No offense, but Jeremy's form isn't exactly macho meat head. More props to him for pursuing something despite his lean figure.

"Yeah," Jeremy says with a chuckle. "I know I'm not the most jacked, and it sounds weird and vain, but I don't know. I just enjoy giving myself a challenge and succeeding at something without having to open my mouth."

"Open your mouth?" she asks.

"I'm not the best with my words. I usually make a fool of myself."

She scoots in closer, her skin nearly grazing his. "I happen to like the things that come out of your mouth." *Yeah, the things I tell him to say,* I say to myself.

Surprisingly, he doesn't tense. He moves closer, tucking a loose strand of hair behind her ear. "What a coincidence, because I like the things that come out of your mouth too." The two are so close. The unopened picnic basket sitting next to them, their breath heavy. Are they going to kiss? This is going so much faster than I anticipated. Something sours in me, maybe it's jealousy, anger that I'm not the one who set this up. A part of me wants to stop it, demand their first kiss be on my orders so I can feel like I have a part, but the moment's too thick, sucking me in. I can't help but lean forward as well, eager for the taste of her lips on mine. But then thunder shakes the ground around us, and Charlotte pulls back. Sloppy, wet raindrops fall all around us.

Chapter Seven

Jeremy

I stand, head swiveling around like an idiot, water blurring the world around me.

"You didn't check the forecast?" Ramsay barks over the patter of downpour.

"No! You didn't tell me to," I yell, clearly not thinking.

"What?" Charlotte asks, her voice straining.

"Shut up, you idiot!" Ramsay shouts in a hushed yell. "Grab her hand and the picnic. Take her under the falls." What would I do without a rat on my head? Wait for the water to carry us away, my mouth gobbling drops like a bass? Thank God he's here. I trust this rat with my life at this point. "Come on," I yell, pulling Charlotte along.

"Where are we going?"

"Somewhere dry. Hopefully," I reply, skipping over rocks, being careful that she doesn't trip as I lead   her along.

I don't know how he could see it from the mesh lining in my hat, but he was right. We make it into a small divot on the other side of the streaming water, covered by rock formations above. The circular space echoes with the sound of the outside rain, and the crashing water envelops us. I let go of Charlotte, crouching to catch my breath, holding myself up on my bent knees. Charlotte's laughter permeates through the crashing rain outside our rocky shelter. She twirls at the center of the cave, her wet skirt splashing water around her.

Momentarily, I'm lost in her beauty—amazed she isn't fuming that she's soaking wet and still without a bite of food, but then I feel like shit because of course, this is all my fault. "I'm sorry. I should have looked at the forecast before," I say, setting down the picnic basket on the stone floor.

"Don't be silly. This is so much more fun." She wrings out her hair and gazes at me with a giddy smile.

My cheeks burn from my own grin, and although I can't see Ramsay's expression, I can't imagine a universe where someone's not completely enamored by such a beautiful sight as the one before us. He's a man after all, just in the body of a rat. There's no chance he could be immune to her charm.

"Here, I can dry you off a bit." I hand her the checkered picnic blanket, and I'm thankful I remembered to grab it before we fled for cover. It's not much drier than either of us, but she accepts my offering as I help wrap it around her shoulders. "Thanks." She stares up at me, her eyes brown, beautiful saucers.

Electricity zips between us, the small space around us alight with energy. Her breath hitches as we move closer. I must be reading this wrong. I've only behaved like an idiot in her presence, with a few sprinkles of genius with the help of Ramsay. There's no way she could want me even a fraction of the amount that I want her. But her eyes droop and her lips part. The signals are there, and I don't need a rat's guidance to read her desire. I lean in on my own accord, but a whisper comes from above. "Kiss her." The order electrifies my blood even more.

Our lips collide, and the world falls away. It's slow at first, but then our mouths move around each other, and soft noises escape her lips. The sounds stiffen my cock to a painful level. I'm momentarily self-conscious of my erection pressed against her wet frame.

Charlotte allows the blanket to fall off her shoulders and presses herself harder against me, her pebbled breasts grazing against my chest. It's almost too much, the friction just starting, but already there's a roaring fire in my abdomen.

Her sounds grow louder, our kisses deepen, and our hands roam each other's backs. It's just the two of us, floating in an endless abyss of pleasure, until a low rumble brings me back to reality. "Touch her breast," Ramsay whispers.

I straighten, the order awakens something primal and hidden inside of me, but the rational part of my brain can't help but wonder if it's the right thing to do. It's so forward and not gentlemanly to do on the first date, but she's practically begging for it, her hands gripping tighter around my neck as she rubs herself against me.

Before I can make my decision, my hand moves on its own accord, dragging up her side so gently it hurts. Ramsay's taking the lead now, directing me. I lean into it, my body turning light from the absence of the impossible choice.

Charlotte pulls her chest away slightly, allowing access to her full breasts. Her hardened nipples poke through the thin material of her wet tank top. The bottom half of her stays glued to me. My cock throbs, nearly stabbing her.

My hand moves up her side until it reaches the beginning of her mound. She presses into my touch, begging for me to grab her, tease her, please her. Ramsay doesn't resist, dragging my finger gently over her nipple.

"Oh, God." She moans. She wants this. It doesn't matter that we barely know each other. This hushed moment takes us out of our forms, leaving us nothing but two aching souls yearning to fit together.

Ramsay pinches her nipple, and she grinds harder against me. "Jesus Christ," I murmur against her lips. Something about having my body used like a puppet rewires my brain. I want Ramsay to use me at his will, to pleasure her, and maybe even to please himself, as fucked up as it sounds.

"Yes, don't stay silent." His words are tortured as if he feels the same euphoria zipping through my veins. I nearly burst inside my pants.

Ramsay   releases   my hand, and I take charge, pinching her nipple. Ramsay pulls another strand of hair, bringing up my other hand, grabbing her breast with a kneading motion. We're both doing this. We're in this together.

This time her moans aren't soft, instead echoing off the stone walls around us. A small cry comes from above me, and a warm wetness seeps against my scalp. It takes me out of the moment, just for a second, but Charlotte notices. She pulls back, her breath heavy and her face flushed. "We should stop," she says with a smile.

I want to get down on my knees, beg her to let me taste between her legs, but I'm not an animal. I gather myself. "Yeah, you're probably right." I take a step back, even as my cock yells at my brain.

Whether Ramsay agrees or not—and right now, he's radio silent—Charlotte is right. If I want this to be a long-term thing, we have to get to know each other better. And Charlotte—well, she's a long-term type of girl, I can already tell.

"How about you come over to my place for dinner tomorrow night?" she asks, completely breaking the tension around us.

"Yeah, that sounds great," I reply, looking out over the stream through the waterwall to distract from my quaking hands. This is good. Tomorrow is a new chance. "I think it's stopped raining. Wanna head back to our cars?"

"Yeah, that sounds great," Charlotte replies. I don't miss the shudder in her voice and the clenching of her fists.

I scoop the basket from the ground, offer my hand, and we walk out interlinked into the damp midday. I focus on my steps, needing to get back to my car so I can drive home as quickly as possible. Not before I ditch the rat in my hat. I've got some personal business to attend to, something that shouldn't be done in the company of others. Well, that's not true. I'd love to have some guidance—a watchful eye—as I take care of myself, but that would be weird, of course.

Chapter Eight

Charlotte

"Why would I invite him here?" It's probably the hundredth time I've asked myself this question, and yet I still don't have a great answer. My place is a mess, which is very unlike me. Of course, Jeremy will understand. I just moved here and haven't had the time to unpack. Plus, the flimsy, cheap furniture I ordered online is a lot harder to set up than I anticipated. Maybe Jeremy will offer to help me, but that would be horrible, because I don't want him focused on my dresser with a   strange Swedish name, I want him focused on me.

Jeremy is one of the most confusing men I've ever met—which isn't saying a lot since I haven't met lots of men—but I can't help being thrilled by whatever version of him I'll get. One second, he's nervous, and I can't tell if he wants to run away from me or not, and the next, he stares deep into my eyes and makes me feel seen and wanted. It's almost like he's two different men, fighting for one body. I can't say the uncertainty of who I'll get doesn't thrill me.

Yesterday's date went way too far. I know nothing about this man and yet I rubbed myself against him, practically begging him to pull me to the stone floor and fuck me under the waterfall. This is probably a normal reaction. I've spent my whole life sheltered and my first chance of freedom makes me want to do all the naughty things I've never gotten to do.

Jeremy is a sweet guy. I trust him enough in my apartment. A fuck to clear my head wouldn't be the worst idea. My mind is so clouded by his looks that I can't decide if he's actually a guy I'd want to date or not. Once we bang it out, I'll be able to assess properly.

I should have made dinner, but I figured ordering Chinese would be enough, considering my plans don't revolve around eating. The doorbell rings just as I pull out the last cardboard carton and place it on my kitchen table. I check my hair for the millionth time in the mirror in the front entryway and blow out my nerves before pulling open the door. "Hi," I say, taking in the man before me, just as gorgeous as the day before. In fact, there's a lot about his appearance that's similar to yesterday. He wears a different shirt, a baby blue, linen button-down that brings out the otherworldly hue of his eyes. I'm pretty sure his hat is exactly the same.

"Hi," he replies, handing me a bouquet of roughly cut wildflowers. "These are for you."

I blush. "Thank you." He really is the sweetest. Maybe this could be more than a simple lay. I don't want to get my hopes up. It's much too soon to tell.

We stand awkwardly in the threshold. His eyes track aimlessly in his skull as if decoding a message. It's me who's weird, though. "Oh, I'm sorry! Come on in." I motion toward the small one-bedroom apartment behind me. I'm lucky to find such a good place, and conveniently, it's located right above For the Plot Books—one of my favorite places—and only a short walk to Ratcliff's. But right now, I'm feeling self-conscious of how small it is, not to mention the mess.

"Sorry. I haven't had time to unpack. All that I've needed is my desk to work and my bed." I laugh nervously.

Jeremy walks in, examining the place. "No, don't worry. It's all organized chaos. I like it. I'd love to help you unpack." He turns back to me, smiling—it's adorable—with his hands on his hips.

God, I can't take it anymore. I must get him out of his clothes. I charge him and his eyes widen in shock for a moment, but once my lips meet his, he melts into me, running his big strong hands up my back. I push my tongue into his mouth, eager to taste him again. Yesterday wasn't nearly enough. I came home from our date and masturbated as if it was my first time in centuries. I couldn't stop thinking about his hands on my breasts, his shallow breaths, his gruff words.

I reach for his buttons, working from the top, but he stops, pulling away from my lips. He laughs. "Are you sure you want to do this so fast? I can wait until after dinner if you want."

"Fuck dinner. Maybe you can wait, but I can't." I push him into my bedroom. He laughs against my lips, holding me firmly, even as he falls against my bed. I straddle him, immediately caught off guard by his reverent look as he stares up at me. "You're so beautiful," he says. "I can't believe a girl like you would want to do this with me."

His words transform me into another person, someone who's unafraid of their sexuality, someone who's ready to scream their pleasure at the top of their lungs, be damned if the bookshop below can hear her. I grab the bottom of my cotton shirt, rolling it slowly over my abdomen, then my breasts, my eyes locked firmly on his. His pupils blow out, and I swear he murmurs soft praise to himself. Is this what it's like to fuck without the confines of hurrying or fearing getting caught? It hasn't even started yet, and I feel as if I'm already near my edge.

The air pricks my hardened nipples, begging for friction. I pull up Jeremy's shirt and he leans forward, his abs flexing as he assists me in pulling his shirt overhead. God is he devastating—something like an ancient Greek statue, cut from marble. I want to lick every inch of his defined chest, his protruding abs, the perfect V pointing down to the part I'm most interested in.

Please don't have a small dick, I plead in my head. He's too perfect. Something has to be wrong. I just hope he has a shitty personality instead of it being anything with his body. Right now is purely carnal, regret for   my wicked thoughts comes later.

I can't take the anticipation anymore, I reach into his slacks, underneath his tight boxer briefs, and clasp around his hardened length, begging to be free.

"Fuck!" He moans, throwing his head back. My eyes shift from his beautiful face to his package as I release him. There must be a God and I must be one of his favorites, because his dick is perfect. Large—almost dangerously so—lined with veins and a shade of pink that   matches his pouty lips. Speaking of lips, I can't help but want to bring his dick to mine. I haven't eaten after all, and my mouth yearns to be full. I must go slow, his tip already leaks with pre   cum, and from the veins popping at the side of his neck and his clenched eyes—almost like he's in pain—I figure he's not far from his breaking point. Look at us, barely just beginning, and it's already too much. We're like two horny little teenagers.

I run my hands up his chiseled stomach as I bring my mouth to his searing heat, moaning as I roll my lips over him. He grabs the back of my head, massaging my scalp as I take him deeper. It feels so good that I can't help but let my hands wander into the dampness underneath my skirt. My moans increase around his cock and his grip tightens, almost like a punishment, like I'm making things too difficult for him. I quiet, because I'm nothing if not a people pleaser. I don't want him to finish in my mouth—even if I yearn for the powerful feeling of making him come so quickly. No, I want him balls deep, stretching me until I forget who I am. The only sounds are my mouth bopping up and down on his dick, and... it's almost like a squeaking. It's an odd sex noise, but it doesn't turn me off, not even a little bit. I kind of like it.

Jeremy jerks me up by my hair. I pop off him, shocked and desperate for more. I don't even have time to beg because he's sitting up, his lips crashing against mine in an instant. He kisses me deeply, pulling me closer until I'm straddling his lap. His lips move away from my mouth, running down the side of my neck. One hand grabs my breast while the other reaches under my skirt. He runs his fingers through my seam, parting me, teasing me slightly, until he focuses on my clit. "No panties, just for me?" he says, less of a question, more like praise.

I throw my head back, letting him have his way with me. How does he know how to touch me so perfectly? It's like someone's whispering in his ear, informing him of my deepest desires. The squeaking happens again. It takes me out of it for a moment, and I realize he's still wearing his baseball hat—the one he wore yesterday.

I know he isn't bald. The first two times I saw him at the restaurant, his golden mop of hair beckoned me like a beacon from the gods. Maybe he's just too caught up in the moment to take it off. His pressure increases on my sensitive bud, and my attention returns to the melted butter that is the insides of my body.

I position my hips up, spreading my legs wider and allowing him more access. He takes my lead, driving his finger into my entrance, all while continuing to massage my clit. It's perfect. It's exactly what I need, and in seconds, I'm screaming, clinging to him, jerking my hips as my orgasm washes over me in a beautiful burst of pleasure.

He barely lets the euphoria pass before flipping me back against the bed. He stops for a moment, reaching for his pants at the foot of the bed. I realize what he's doing. "I'm on the pill," I say, reaching for him, "And recently got tested."

"Me too," he says, exhaling, falling over me in an instant.

Just like that, I'm no longer sated. I reach between us, needing him inside me. He helps position himself at my entrance. I want him to pound into me, but I know it will hurt like a mother fucker if he does. It's a pain I'm willing to bear, but as I pull myself down on him, using his shoulders as support, he stops me. His hand wraps around my throat. It isn't rough or suffocating, but firm, growing softer as I stop moving and let him take the lead.

He slowly slides into me, stretching me to what I believe is my max with each tiny thrust. His hand doesn't leave my neck, and his mouth trails kisses above his thumb. His thrusts grow deeper, and my need swells with each inch. Finally, after what feels like forever, he reaches his hilt. He pauses for a second, catching his breath. "You fit me so good," he says against my skin.

"Fuck me hard," I beg, and I only need to ask once. He pulls himself out, ramming against me in one fast pump. I cry out, my vision blurring, but it feels so good. "Yes, just like that." I hold onto him, needing his sturdy frame to keep me on in this dimension. He loses himself, thrusting without restraint. He bursts inside of me, murmuring noises and nonsensical phrases. He must have fucked me silly, because as he allows part of his weight to fall against me and as we both sigh in contentment, I swear I hear three sighs.

Chapter Nine

Ramsay

God, do I miss opposable thumbs. Surprisingly, it's the first rat-loathing thought I've had all day—a new record. I'm writing my third letter to Charlotte, not signed by me, of course, but I don't mind pretending to be someone I'm not. If anything, it makes being a rat more bearable. Except for the time it takes me to complete these love letters, due to the previously mentioned lack of appendages. But really, I should be thankful . It's not like I have a busy schedule as a rat.

Jeremy is closing tonight, and although it's a risk to let him operate on the dining floor on his own, I've got more pressing work to do. Charlotte's been here for two hours, sitting by herself at her usual table, making goo-goo eyes at Jeremy as he slips her notes in between his runs. I can't talk to her, only through Jeremy, who usually butchers my intended delivery, but these letters are a way to show Charlotte how I truly feel.

Being part of their coupling two days before was nothing like I've ever experienced. Well, duh. Who can say they controlled a man having sex with the woman he thinks he's starting to fall in love with, but still I never expected it to be so good for me. Maybe it's selfish and taking things too far, but I want more out of this. I can't please her with my own cock, but I can make her panties wet with my words.

The first letter was sweet and short, letting her know how beautiful she looks tonight and that I can't stop thinking about her. The second was almost a ballad—comparing her beauty to that of a starlit night, her smile to the first blink of the morning sun—shit like that. This last one, though, I'm getting a little riskier. I know she'll love it. I thought I had her pinned—that she was a quiet, introspective woman—and those things may be true, but the way she rode my cock—I mean, Jeremy's cock—she is a sex goddess either from the pits of hell or the gates of heaven, maybe both.

That dress. Charlotte, did you wear it to torture me? I scurry down the hall, note in my mouth, landing on Jeremy's shoulder. He doesn't even turn to me, filling up drinks as he grabs it and places it in his pocket. I watch as he nonchalantly places the letter on her table as he passes by.

I hide in the rafters, my rat dick throbbing as I watch her read my words. Her cheeks blush, and she hides her smile behind her hand. She grabs her pen off the table and writes something under my writing, folding it and pushing it toward the edge of the table. Jeremy picks it up as he walks by, and I'm running back to the server station, my heart pounding as I retrieve my letter. I'm surprised he doesn't care to read what we're writing back and forth. Maybe he's letting me have this one thing by myself.

Is it so hideous?

I grin. She's clever. It's obvious she knows what she's doing.

You could wear a potato sack and make it look designer. Although I'd much rather you wear nothing at all.

Our notes are exchanged, and I can nearly feel the heat radiating off her.

I could make that happen. Tomorrow night?

Somehow, this is all more thrilling than texting or talking—the anticipation, a delicious torture.

I pass Jeremy the next note. *Dinner at my place? We could make something together.* It's not what either of us have in mind, but if I want her to keep us around, we must do more than fucking, as much as I don't want to.

It's nine o'clock. The restaurant is closed, and Jeremy and another server are the only people on the floor. Instead of returning my note with a response, Charlotte stands just as Jeremy walks past. She whispers something to him, pulling him close. He grins and nods, mouthing something I can't make out. I have to look away. It hurts too much.

The clock strikes eleven. Jeremy's the last one here, wiping down surfaces as his penance for being new. I meet him on the table.

"So now we're making dinner tomorrow, huh?" He shakes his head, staring down at his rag.

"What, are you disappointed?"

He meets my gaze. "No. It's just I wish I knew what *I* was planning with Charlotte before she approaches me with the details." He rubs at an imaginary spot with increased vigor. Someone is salty.

"Well, now you know." I lie on my side, propping up my head with my hand. "I was thinking, tomorrow night, we need to work on making sure she comes more than once."

He chokes on his saliva. He hits his chest and chuckles. "Yeah, okay," he shakes his head and returns to wiping down the already clean table.

"I'm serious."

He slams the rag down, leaning against the table and glaring at me. "Jesus Christ, were you ever really a human? That's only possible in pornos."

I laugh, sitting up straight. "You're joking, right? You've never made a woman come more than once?"

"I mean, yes, but not during the same... you know, *session.*"

"No, I don't know. I bet you've slept with way more women than me, but even I made a woman come from foreplay and then around my cock."

He scoffs. "Why would you assume I've slept with more women than you?"

"Have you seen yourself?" The room tightens as Jeremy's pupils grow. It's not a secret that Jeremy is attractive—anyone with eyes can see it, but saying it out loud, our faces nearly touching, and after everything we've done together, it makes things much heavier than they should be.

I watch him, study every minuscule movement, waiting for his next move. I nearly forget I'm a rat. Instead, I'm a human soul, outside of my body, waiting for the other part of the tether I just threw out to the roaring sea.

Jeremy doesn't forget, though. He's the one staring at my rodent body. He blinks rapidly, smiling and returning to his cleaning. "Whatever, if you want to try to make her come tomorrow night, be my guest, I'm a vessel at your disposal." He means to lighten the mood, make things more casual, but that's the problem—his words never come out as he intends them to. Unless they do and he's fighting to share his true meaning.

I'm aroused, painfully so. It's obvious Jeremy wants this tension to end, but I'm not there yet. "The next thing you're going to tell me is that you've never made yourself come more than once in a *session.*"

He laughs. "Come on, dude. Now I know you're fucking with me."

"I bet I could show you how to come multiple times." It's not subtle this time. I've said the words that there's no going back from. I've enjoyed controlling Jeremy, using his body to act on my passions, but I can't deny my   primal attraction toward him.

He obviously doesn't feel the same way—I'm a rat—but I can't help but notice his breath slowing, his eyelid drooping slightly as if letting the weight of my words settle over him. The moment is gone as quickly as it came. He pushes it away. "Whatever, man. I'm going home. I'm tired." He turns to walk away, not before calling back. "I'll be here at four tomorrow to pick you up for our date."

I watch him go. I know what he means, but I can't help hoping that there's more weight to his words.

Chapter Ten

Jeremy

I can't believe it. My apartment looks nothing like it did two hours ago. It should have been evident that the art my mom gave me from her travels to Greece would look better on the wall above my table instead of shoved in   the back of my closet, but decorating has never been my forte. And the candles hidden in the back of the cabinet above the stove—who would have thought they still smelled like pine and could give   the small apartment a warm glow?

I picked Ramsay up from the restaurant early today because I needed some help getting ready for my date with Charlotte. I figured he'd assist me in organizing the pizza toppings I bought for our meal, but that little rat had much bigger plans, most of them involving turning my space from a sad bachelor's pad into a love interest's swanky chateau in a steamy rom-com. Okay, maybe I'm giving my straightened-up home a little too much credit, but color me impressed.

After our fight—or whatever it was—at Ratcliff's last night, I was starting to reconsider this relationship. Of course, it's unconventional, but I never anticipated things would get this unhinged. I've never previously been attracted to men, and he isn't even a man on the outside. I don't find his furry appearance appealing, I'm not a sicko, but his words, the way he knows what I want without me having to speak—I can't deny it does something to me. It's all too much, and this can't go on forever, but after seeing what he did with my space—I might need him more than I thought. Charlotte isn't just a hook up. As much fun as fucking her was, I want more. I want her, for real, and if that's possible, I need Ramsay.

"What time is it?" Ramsay asks, carefully rearranging the mini pickles on the charcuterie board. I don't have the heart to ask if he washed his paws.

I glance at my watch. "5:30   "

"Shit, she'll be here any minute."

"Dude, calm down. The place is perfect." I motion to the expertly-lit room around me. The island counter   top is dressed with powdered pizza dough, small white bowls filled with toppings, and two full glasses of wine—Pinot Noir, of course.

A knock sounds from the door.

"Shit, shit, shit. Put me on your head!" Ramsay yells, scrambling up my arm.

I sigh, grabbing him from my shoulder and placing my trusty baseball cap over him. I'm not nearly as nervous as he is, but I guess I'm not the one who has to think too hard during this date.

"You're going to need a new hat. This one is getting old."

I shake my head, not willing to argue about how hats can't be a forever solution. I pull the door open, and my balance is knocked off-   kilter. I just saw her yesterday, but she's stunning—wearing a thin-strapped red dress, revealing all her curves and offering an ample view of the top of her full breasts.

"Say, hi. Idiot."

"Hi!" I blink back to reality. "I'm sorry, come on in."

Before she enters, she points to my head, and I quiver. "What's with the hat?"

"What do you mean?"

"You wore it for our last date? Is it lucky or something?"

Shit. I'm hoping Ramsay is thinking fast because I've got nothing. "Tell her you're growing out your hair and it keeps it out of your face."

I repeat his words, and she scrunches her face as she registers. She doesn't buy it completely, but I doubt she suspects I'm hiding a talking rat. She doesn't press more. Instead, her head swivels as she takes in my surroundings. "Wow, your   place looks great. Much better than my mess."

I don't want her to feel bad about herself. My place was a bit of a mess only two hours ago, but I can't tell her that. "How about I come over later this week and help you put your place together? I've suddenly developed a knack for organizing and decorating."

"That sounds perfect." She grabs my hand, pulling it to her chest. I can feel her heartbeat quickening. I don't need a rat in my ear to read the look on her face. She wants something from me, and it's not food. But then a rat does whisper in my ear, ruining the moment. "Food first," he orders.

I step back. "I thought it would be fun if we made our own pizzas." I motion to the countertop.

She shakes her head, ridding herself of the steam in her eyes. "That sounds amazing." She walks over, picking up the glass of wine and taking a sip. "And you got my favorite. Man, are you sweet. I'd say you're trying to get in my pants, but it's obvious I won't make that a difficult task." She smirks at me over her glass, the liquid inside draining. *Fuck.* I might have to ditch the rat and have her here on this countertop. I don't think either of us can wait until after dinner.

"I can feel your dick throbbing. Cool it," Ramsay orders. "Put an apron on her."

"Here, I don't want you to get your dress dirty." I grab the red material off the back of a stool and she turns for me to put it over her head, slightly rubbing her ass into my crotch. I groan but take a step back to tie her waistband. She twirls. "How do I look?"

I shake my head, putting my green apron on. I don't have words. Thankful Ramsay does. "Tell her, you'd tell her, but then you worry it will just make your pants tighter after seeing the shocked look on her face." *Geez,* but I do what he says.

It has the intended effect. Her cheeks heat, her eyes grow, and her lips part. My crotch becomes increasingly painful. It's like this fucking rat is edging me. He doesn't want to let me take her now, but he'll order me to say the most suggestive things until I'm at the point of pain.

I clap my hands. "Alright, let's make some pizza."

Truth is, the pizza wasn't my idea. Surprise, surprise. Ramsay stops me from dumping a whole bowl of olives on top of an already generous amount of pineapple. "Calm down. She's going to think you're a psycho if you put that many toppings on. Stick with some ham and call it a day." Now this guy is telling me what to eat? If only he had a passion for fitness and nutrition, my life would be perfect.

I look at Charlotte's pizza as she carefully places a slice of onion. Her food looks more like a work of art. All the toppings are evenly distributed. "Done," she says, taking one last look at her creation with her hands on her hips.

The oven beeps behind us. "Perfect timing." I place both of our pizzas in the oven. When I glance back toward Charlotte—she's sitting on top of the counter, wine glass empty, lips dark red, devouring me with her gaze. "What should we do until they're done?" she asks, and I know for certain she already has something in mind.

"Slowly walk toward her, push her legs apart, pull her panties to the side and eat her pussy." It sounds so vulgar coming from his mouth, but it's actually what my dick begs me to do.

"I have an idea," I say in a low, husky tone, walking toward her.

Her chest heaves as I approach, and when I gently touch her knee, she sighs, shuddering. God, Ramsay was right. She's so aroused. The anticipation nearly kills her as I get closer, my eyes not leaving her face as my hands trail up the smooth skin of her thighs. I push myself in between her legs, and she welcomes me, reaching for me when I'm pressed against her.

I want to give in to her demands, allow my throbbing cock to rub against her cunt as her lips meet mine, but Ramsay stops me, the bastard. He pushes her back, using my body as a vessel for his wish. She studies me curiously until I slowly drop to my knees. She lies down on the granite, spreading her legs wide for me.

"Gently now. Slowly move those juicy panties to the side," Ramsay whispers. I do as he says. Last time, I didn't get a chance to appreciate this part of her body. Sure, I felt its glorious effects as she gripped my cock, but now I get to see the true beauty between her legs. I could kiss that damned rat.

"Now blow on her cunt. I want to see it clench." I watch in pure wonder as her legs shake and her pussy seeps more liquid. "Jeremy!" she cries out. God, he knows her well. She's so wet, I can't help but bring my mouth to the velvety skin.

Ramsay tugs on my hair. "Not yet!" But I fight against him, needing her taste on my tongue. Charlotte cries from above me as I increase my tempo, trailing my tongue up and down her tender valleys. Her noises heighten, and she reaches between her legs and grabs my hair. I'm too lost, my cock dripping inside my jeans. I don't stop until I hear her scream.

I jerk up, assessing her. She's terrified, bringing her legs onto the counter and pulling into herself. "What's wrong?" I ask.

"There's a rat on your head!"

I pat my uncapped head, realizing she must have knocked off my hat when she reached for my hair. "Oh, that's Ramsay, don't worry about it." I'm still not thinking clearly, my dick taking all the blood from my head.

"What? You know there's a rat on your head?" She gets on all fours, scooting backwards off the counter.

"You're an idiot," Ramsay says with a sigh.

She screams so loud I'm sure my neighbors will call the police. I grab Ramsay and place him on the counter, moving toward her. "Charlotte, calm down. He's not really a rat. He's a man trapped in a rat body."

She shakes her head, backing toward the door. "I knew Ghostlight Falls had some odd occurrences, but this is too much."

"Charlotte, wait. He's been helping me. I just like you so much, and so does he, and he's better at words and actions. I just needed some guidance."

"I think that's a little too much information, buddy." We both look toward Ramsay at the counter. "But Charlotte, trust me, I had big plans for you tonight. You would have appreciated this partnership," he says.

She shakes her head. "This is too fucking weird. I'm going home." She races toward the front door.

"Charlotte, no wait. I can explain more."

"Goodbye, Jeremy," she says, slamming the door in my face.

The oven beeps. "Looks like the pizza is done," Ramsay says from behind me as I rest my forehead against the peephole.

The girl of my dreams is gone—probably never wants to see me again. And now I'm all alone, incredibly   horny and my only company is an equally horny rat.

Chapter Eleven

Ramsay

I no longer trust my judgment. I'm as clueless as Jeremy. I could have played it smarter when Charlotte ripped off Jeremy's hat and discovered me. I definitely didn't make things better, that's for sure. Now, as I stand outside Charlotte's apartment—completely alone with a small bouquet of wild flowers clutched in my paw, I'm sure I've gone completely mad.

I'm probably the last person—rat—she wants to see, but I can't stomach the idea of not apologizing. I crossed a line, intruded where I was not welcome, and Charlotte didn't deserve that. I didn't think of this as an invasion until I witnessed her adverse reaction. Maybe living as vermin for a time has rotted my brain.

Thankfully, Charlotte's apartment is right across the street from Ratcliff's, but still, it took me several hours to get here. Crossing a street, dodging cars, and avoiding being stomped on by gremlins (literally) is a much more challenging task for a rat in the light of day. I had to speak to her in daylight, though. Rats are less welcome in the dark.

I stare up at her front door, after scurrying through the back alleyway of the bookstore and thankfully, catching the door to the hallway ajar. My luck has run out, though, because no matter how hard I knock, Charlotte will never hear me.

If there's a weird, demented God up there, I must have his favor at this moment, because right when I'm about to give up, the door swings open. "Wait!" I yell before I'm toppled by Charlotte exiting her apartment. She screams, scanning for the source of the sound. "Jesus Christ, not you!" she says, exasperated once her eyes catch mine.

"Listen, I know I'm the last person you want to see right now, but I came by to apologize and give you these." I hold out the flowers.

"You're not the last person I want to see."

My spirit lightens. "Really?"

"You're the last rat I want to see." She steps into her apartment, attempting to separate us with her door.

"Wait!" Surprisingly, she heeds my plea. "Can I help you set up your apartment? It's the least I can do after everything."

She stops, her head turning into her home behind her. "Fine." I can hardly believe it. "But I don't know how you'll be able to do much. You're a rat, after all." She steps out of the way, keeping the door open for me.

I can't deny that the words sting, but I don't blame her. She doesn't know me. To her, I'm the creepy little rodent that stared into the depths of her vagina, and okay, maybe I am that, but I'm also so much more. I greedily accept her invitation, darting in and getting to work.

After only two hours, her place looks brand new. Her couch has two assembled side tables. The boxes in her kitchen are unpacked, and cooking supplies are in their designated drawers. I even managed to hang up some art by crawling across the walls, and put my small bouquet into a teacup with water. I have no plans to stop anytime soon.

"So you're a man, not just a talking rat?" Charlotte's eyes haven't left me since I entered, but this is the first time she's spoken.

I nod, placing a small picture frame back into a box to give her my full attention. "My name is Ramsay." I can't believe this is the first time I'm telling her that. "I was a soldier at Fort Pines. I stupidly volunteered to be a part of a science experiment and woke up as a rat. I escaped. I'm not supposed to be alive."

"Are you going to be a rat forever?"

I shrug. "I think so. I overheard the scientists say they didn't have any way to turn me back into a man."

"Aren't you worried they're coming after you?" She's closer to me now, sitting at the bar stool in front of me.

I shake my head. "They wrote me off as dead. Said I wouldn't escape the facility, and if I did, I wouldn't survive in the outside world. I don't think I was supposed to retain my intelligence or talk."

She's quiet, studying me. "So what? Jeremy's your best friend, and you both take part in luring women into your weird sex fetishes?"

"No!" I almost yell, but quickly soften, realizing this is a logical conclusion. "I barely know Jeremy. I've been hiding out at Ratcliff's and watching people. It's one of my favorite pastimes."

"Mine too."

I smile. "I figured."

Something passes between us—a warm glance, something heated—but Charlotte shakes it away. "Okay, tell me how this all happened."

I tell her as much as I can—how Jeremy and I met, how it evolved, the mechanics of how I helped.

"I still don't get it," she says. "Why do you care?"

"Care about what?"

"Jeremy? Me? Did you just need something to waste time on?"

"No, it was never that."

"Then what?"

"It was you. The first time I saw you, I could tell you were someone special. Then, you kept coming in, and I studied you, learning more about you than you wanted anyone to know. I could never have you, and I accepted that, but when I saw Jeremy and you looked at him the way I wished you looked at me, I decided that if I couldn't have you, I'd help him, because above everything, you deserved to be happy."

She's silent, stunned speechless, and for the first time since she walked through the front door of Ratcliff's, I can't read her. Her lips part. "So the letter, all of it was you, not Jeremy?"

"The letters were me, and yes, I helped him with his words and... actions, but he truly cares about you, and he's a good guy. At first, this was just about you, but it slowly became about you both." My skin heats. My words are too close to a confession.

Something washes over Charlotte's expression—understanding. She senses my discomfort, carrying on the conversation. "So now what?"

"What do you mean?"

"How do you want this to carry on?"

I chuckle. "It's not about me; it never should have been. I thought I was helping to bring the two of you together, but I was wrong. I overstepped. I intruded on your privacy. You don't have to worry about me anymore, but Jeremy, I think you should give him another chance."

She nods. The weight in my heart heavies. Of course, I want her to say no, that this could work somehow, but that's a fantasy. I was never truly part of this, and I will never be anything more. I'm a rat—vermin. I'll stay hidden in the shadows until I die a lowly death. It's time I come to terms with that.

"I should go."

She nods, her eyes watery.

I don't look back as I crawl across the floor and exit through the small crack of her ajar front door.

Chapter Twelve

Charlotte

It hasn't even been five minutes since Ramsay left when someone's knocking on my door. For a moment, I think he could be back, but I remember he's a rat. There's no way he could knock on my door and actually make a sound.

When I pull it open and see Jeremy, I can't help the warm feeling filling my stomach. I should be furious at him, which I am, but I also can't help associating him with pleasure. I don't greet him, just cross my arms over my chest, glaring at him. I should slam the door in his face, but after Ramsay's apology, I can't help that I'm softened toward the situation.

A normal person, in a normal town, would probably be sent to a mental hospital after finding out her lover had a talking rat controlling him and learning that said rat was really a man transformed into a rat, but this is Ghostlight Falls. This kind of shit is normal. I've only lived here a few weeks and I already know that. It doesn't make any of this okay, though.

"Charlotte, I'm sorry." He's empty-handed. Although he looks his normal devastatingly handsome self, his curly locks are disheveled and his clothes are wrinkled. It's clear to me now the difference between

Ramsay's guidance and his absence. "Can I come in?" His expression is defeated.

I wait, making him sweat, but of course I open the door, motioning for him to enter. "Wow, it looks great in here," he says.

"Wasn't me."

He freezes, studying me. "Ramsay?" A part of me wondered if they were working together for this apology. Jeremy isn't wearing a hat, so unless they've come up with a different hiding spot, he's solo. But still, this could have been rehearsed. From the genuine quizzical look on his face, I can tell that's not the case.

"Yep."

"Is he here?"

I plop onto the couch, my arms still over my chest. "You just missed him. I'm curious to see how you behave without your leader."

He rushes to me, sits on the couch, and grabs my hand. "Charlotte, believe me, if I thought I could gain your affection on my own, I'd do it. It seemed like the only way."

I scoff. "So you thought the only option was letting a rat guide you instead of, I don't know, being yourself?"

"You don't understand."

"No, Jeremy, I don't. Please explain to me why you made this choice."

He takes a breath, turning away from me as if to gather his thoughts. "I told you I've never been good with my words. It's like my brain and mouth are on two different settings. I get so nervous that I end up making the shittiest choice. I met you in a place where I was at my worst. I'm a horrible server, and there you were, looking like heaven personified, and I made an idiot of myself in front of you. When Ramsay showed up, I was freaked out, but then he gave me some tips, and it worked. I knew it wouldn't be enough, though. I'd fuck up and you'd want nothing to do with me."

I reach out, grabbing his arm. "You're being too harsh. Have you seen yourself? I'm sure girls swoon over you all the time."

He turns to me, his eyes sparkling. "Sure, girls notice me, until I open my mouth and say something stupid."

"Is Ramsay controlling you now?"

"No, I promise."

"Well, you're not saying anything stupid now. In fact, you sound pretty sincere."

He smiles, almost boyish, almost like he's not used to the compliment. He takes a deep breath. "Well, now I'm going to ruin it."

"Why?"

"Because I want to tell you the full truth, even if it's fucked up."

My heart beats faster.

"It turned into something else. Sure, I needed the direction, but once I got comfortable with you, I didn't need him as much, but I still wanted him there."

I scoot in closer, genuinely curious, "Why?"

He shrugs. "I think I enjoyed the direction, turning my brain off, especially during sex. But then I think I just enjoyed Ramsay's company." His cheeks heat. "I know he's a rat, but he's also not. He's a man."

I nod. Perhaps I should be more disturbed by his confession. He basically just admitted to being turned on by the sexually deviant rodent on his head, but I can't judge him, mostly because I understand what he's saying. Ramsay was just in my apartment, and from the way he talked to me, I could understand the appeal. But of course, neither of us can act on these thoughts. Regardless of what he is on the inside, he's in the body of the rat, and that's fucked up.

I sigh. "Okay."

He looks at me, shocked. "You're not disturbed?"

"Maybe I should be, but...."

"But what?"

"I still like you." I look away, too embarrassed to meet his gaze. It's wild. This man looked me in the eyes as he sucked my clit just the night before, but things seem more vulnerable now.

"You do?"

"Maybe you're not as bad with your words as you think. Maybe being honest makes you hotter." I meet his gaze, heated and darting from my lips to my eyes. I move forward just a millimeter and he rushes to close the distance, cradling my jaw as he devours my mouth with his. He pulls me onto his lap, and I wrap my arms around his neck.

I grind against his rock-hard cock underneath his pants. I reach for him, the heat pooling between my legs becoming too much, but he stops me. "Wait, I want to finish what I started." I'm confused for only a moment, before he pushes me back, spreading my legs wide and running his fingers up my thighs. He pulls down my thin sleep shorts and panties, throwing them across the room once he gets them over my feet. My breath is as labored as an engine and just watching him rip my clothes off is a form of foreplay.

He kisses up my leg, sending shockwaves through my system. For a moment, my head clears and I wonder if I'm accepting his apology too quickly. Minutes ago, I was furious at him and now his tongue teases my seam. Maybe I'm being too easy, but honestly I don't give a fuck. I'm much too attracted to him, and maybe the rat isn't as weird as I initially thought.

He dives into me, spreading my lips with his fingers as his tongue lathers me up and down before focusing on my clit. He circles the sensitive bud and in seconds, I'm so close to that blinding edge. I grab onto his muscular back, my nails digging into his skin as his name spills from my lips. He pulls back, pulling up my sleep shirt and kissing up to my neck.

I grind against him as he works on unbuttoning his pants and freeing himself from his briefs. The heat of his cock against my stomach is intoxicating. I reach for him, needing him inside of me, but he grabs my hands, holding them both above my head with one of his hands. The other positions his tip at my entrance. "Fuck, Charlotte. I need you." It's desperate, begging almost. He gives shallow thrusts, but I'm already so wet, my body accepting his size readily. He moves deeper, and I nearly lose my mind at the sensation.

He hits the back of me, the delicious spot that sends my toes curling. "Jeremy," I cry out, pulling him closer. His abs rub against my clit as his speed increases. My orgasm barrels through me just moments before he's spurting inside of me. "Fuck!" he cries, not letting up until every last drop is drained.

My body floats back to earth, and Jeremy settles himself on top of me, still holding most of his weight up on the couch. He breathes me in, and I rub a hand down his back.

I'm sated. Satisfied. But I can't help but think that something is missing.

Chapter Thirteen

Jeremy

There was a note underneath my keys when I left the restaurant last night. A rat broke up with me—at least that's what it felt like. He's always so eloquent, and the way he explained how our arrangement couldn't work anymore and that he was leaving me forever, it almost made me understand his reasoning. Almost. But not enough for me not to feel his absence on my shift tonight. I've gotten better at my job—I blame Ramsay—but it doesn't make me wish any less that I didn't have him here with me. Who would have thought that just a few weeks with a rat pulling my hair, I'd be so addicted to his direction?

Even with my improved skills, I'm still tasked with closing down the restaurant. I'm the last one here, but Charlotte should arrive any minute. My side work is done, but I leave one table perfectly set up, complete with a rose centerpiece and a steaming plate of ratatouille. Two plates and glasses of Pinot Noir sit in front of each chair. I light the candle, placing it next to the rose right as Charlotte walks through the front door. "Jeremy?"

"Right here!" I call, waving at her once she catches me.

She's stunning as usual, wearing a simple light blue dress that highlights the creaminess of her skin. "What is this?" she asks, a smile creeping at the corner of her full lips.

"I didn't think my apology at your apartment was good enough. I thought it might be nice to have a private dinner together. I got it cleared by my manager." Ramsay would be proud of my thoughtfulness, and of course, there's a part of me hoping he's watching.

She erases the distance between us, placing her small hands on my chest and bringing her lips to mine. "You're so thoughtful." I don't miss the way her eyes search the top of my head before returning to my gaze. I want to confirm that this plan was all my doing, but I don't want to ruin the moment. I pull out the chair next to me, motioning for her to sit. I place a white napkin on her lap and push her in before taking a seat across from her.

"This is so nice," she says before bringing the wine glass to her lips. I copy her, drinking down the liquid, wishing it were a Diet Coke instead, but pretending to enjoy it. We stare at each other, our eyes darting. Charlotte brings the glass to her lips again.

"I..."

"Do..." We both speak at the same time. Awkward laughter ensues. "You go first," I say.

"No, I was just going to ask if you like ratatouille."

"Oh!" I stare down at the delicately arranged vegetables in   the middle of the table. "Sure." I shrug. Everything at Ratcliff's is delicious, but ratatouille would probably be my last choice. "I know it's your favorite."

She nods. "Yeah. To be fair, I haven't tried much else on the menu."

"Next time I'll have the chef make us something else."

"Oh, no. I didn't mean to sound like I wasn't happy with   the ratatouille."

"No, I know."

She takes another large sip. More uncomfortable silences pass between us. It's never been like this before. It's usually effortless. It's obvious why, though. This is our first date without Ramsay.

Charlotte sighs. "Can I just say something?"

Thank God. "Yeah, of course."

"When I first found out about Ramsay watching and guiding you, I was really freaked out."

"I know, and I'm so sorry..."

"But after talking to him, I could understand how you came to the conclusion to include him."

"Really?"

She grabs my hand from across the table. "I'm not saying that anything is wrong with just you, though. This is nice." *Sure, but nice won't get her panties wet,* I think to myself. "But he's just so commanding, so sure of himself, even as a rat." I don't miss the dreamy filter that drops over her eyes. "I don't blame you for accepting his help."

"You don't?"

She shakes her head. There's still something there, something we're both not saying. We study each other, waiting for the other to break.

"Well, Ramsay left me a note last night, letting me know that he would leave us alone."

"Do you ask him to do that?"

"No. I assumed after his conversation with you, he felt like that was what you wanted."

"What do you want?" She leans forward.

"I want you."

"That's it?"

"I mean, of course, there are other things I want in life, like bodybuilding championships."

"I know that, but I mean in our relationship. Will you be happy with just the two of us?"

I don't have to contemplate. Charlotte is enough. "Of course."

She nods, leaning back in her chair,   something almost like disappointment streaking across her face.

It's time to be brave. "But..."

"But?" She leans forward again.

"But I wouldn't mind it."

"Mind what?"

"If Ramsay was part of this. Like he was before." I tense. This is it. She either agrees with me (unlikely) or is disturbed and out of my life forever. Seconds tick on like centuries, and thoughts move behind her eyes. "I don't mind either."

I can't believe it, but I must know more. Does she feel the same way I do? "Would you prefer it?"

She struggles more to answer this one. Ramsay could be out of our lives together. If we admit this to each other and can't get him back, where does that leave us?

"I think so."

I jerk forward, hands on the table. "You do?"

"The other night, it was nice." There's that damned word again. I'd prefer her to use shitty—it's what she really means. "But it wasn't the same as before."

I nod. "Something was missing."

"Yeah."

We stare at each other for a moment before I pop to my feet. "Let's find that damned rat."

Chapter Fourteen

Ramsay

Of course, I was listening. I nearly fell out of the rafters, hanging on their every word. This was a bad idea. After I wrote that note to Jeremy, I should have left. Sure, Ratcliff's has been a decent enough home, but there are other options in town. Grim's Bakery seemed like a nice place to live. It's close enough and sweet enough to put myself in a daily sugar coma. But I couldn't stop watching him. I can't deny it stung a little to see him do so well on his shifts the past two days. Tonight dug the knife even deeper. He set up a romantic dinner for her. He didn't need me anymore.

But then, but then... that damned confession.

If I were close enough, I could have been able to tell. I could have felt the awkward tension and the unsaid words, but from up high, the revelation came to me as a surprise. They missed me, and now they are both on their hands and knees, calling my name and searching for me in the corners of the restaurant.

A part of me—the selfish part—wants to scurry down the wall and join them in whatever they have in mind, but the quieter part, the one I've learned to listen to in the military, tells me to stay put. They can't rely on me to fill the gaps in their compatibility. I'll always be a rat, and as a rat, I can't be an equal part in their relationship. I should let them tire themselves out, and then I'll leave this restaurant for good.

I just have to get a better look before I go, witness their faces, commit it to memory. I crawl to the floor. Jermey searches through an artificial plant, and Charlotte paces around the dining room, hands on her hips. "I know you're here, Ramsay," she says.

I tense, pushing myself more into the shadow behind the leg of a chair. Can she see me?

"I know you think you're doing the right thing by leaving us, but this could work."

How? I want to scream, but I remain quiet, feeling like she has more to share.

"There are no rules for this. I'm pretty sure you're the first man to be turned into a rat."

Jeremy stands next to her, grabbing her hand. "This is Ghostlight Falls. The weird is accepted here. Maybe we can't have a conventional relationship, but we could make this work, all three of us, together, each of us having an equal part."

"So, tell me how this would work?" They twirl around, facing me on their abandoned dining table as I lounge against Charlotte's empty wine glass.

"Ramsay!" They both exclaim wistfully, rushing toward me.

"You realize I can't be an equal member of this, right? I'm a rat."

Their smiles fade. "Maybe not equal, but we could each have our part," Charlotte says, her brown eyes full of hope. It hurts to see.

"You could be the leader, commanding us to your will. I'd be your vessel, playing out your desires," Jeremy says, stepping closer to me.

I prance around the table, paws behind my back. "And that's it?" I'm being greedy. I should devour this offer. What other chance will I have at being part of any relationship as a rat? I can't help that I want more. I want all of them.

"It wouldn't be just sex," Charlotte says. "You'd be a member of this. Hold your own conversations, share your own thoughts and dreams, not through Jeremy this time."

"Why would you want that?" My heart pounds.

She steps forward, standing above me. "I like you, on the inside."

"But you barely know me."

"But I'd like to know more. You see me more than anyone has ever cared to. You know what I like, and you're confident in yourself, even as a rat. You're someone I want in my life."

I can't form words. I almost wish I had a smaller rat on the top of my head telling me what to do and say next.

Jeremy steps next to Charlotte. "She's not the only one who feels this way. I like you, Ramsay. More than a friend, more than a human should like a rat. If this situation is all we can have, I don't want to be without it."

Tears cloud my vision. Maybe I'm dreaming. None of this feels real. They want me even in my tiny, furry form. Ever since I woke up in the body of a rat, I thought my life was over, but now I see a new—strange—but wonderful beginning for myself. "Okay."

"Okay?" Jeremy asks, hope filling the lines of his face.

I chuckle. "Yes, okay. If you guys don't mind me hanging around, I'll be part of this. Whatever that looks like."

"Oh, Ramsay," Charlotte leans over, kissing me on my furry cheek. It's the first time someone's touched me with affection in God knows how long. My body heats. It's nice, but it immediately drops a heavy stone into my gut. This is it for me. Soft kisses, awkward cuddles, it will be all I'll get from them. But it's good enough, because they're so damned special.

We stare at each other, grinning ear to ear.

"So, now what?" Jeremy asks, and it's so refreshing to see him look to me for his next steps again.

I shrug, the whiff of the food behind me catching my attention. "Let's have a meal together."

"I'd love that," Charlotte says.

Jeremy runs to the other side of the table, taking his seat. They each make themself a plate of the ratatouille, and Jeremy makes a smaller plate for me. It's warm in here, but only from the happiness radiating off us. It's quiet but not like before when it was just the two of them. Now it has a purpose. I take a bite, my mood heightening by the delicious herby taste, but my stomach quickly sours, and my vision blurs until there's nothing but blackness. The last thing I hear is Charlotte and Jeremy calling my name.

Chapter Fifteen

Ramsay

My consciousness blinks. The world opens to me like I'm cracking from a shell. I'm somewhere foreign, lying on a bed and staring up at a popcorn ceiling, a fan blowing cool air on my face. I groan, rubbing my face. My stubble pricks my fingers. Odd since I'm always so well-shaven. Well, except as a rat, of course, there'd be no point.

I jerk up. My heart beats wildly as I bring my hands to my line of vision—my human hands. This must be a dream, or maybe I'm dead and returned to my true form in heaven.

I look around the room. I've been here before. It's a simple, clean space, and a picture of a field of wildflowers hangs next to the door. I hung that picture. It took me forever as a rat.

"Charlotte!" I call, throwing my legs over the bed to stand. I look down. Shit, I'm naked. I grab a pillow from the top of the bed, using it to shield my manhood. Charlotte barges through the door, followed by Jeremy. "Oh my God!" She covers her mouth.

"It's me, Ramsay," I say. She doesn't seem confused by who I am, but how would she know? A disturbing thought pops into my head, and I turn to the floor-length mirror to my side. I take in my reflection, running my hands down my jaw and over my chest. My anxiety deflates. I'm not some rat-human creature. I'm completely back to my normal self. "What happened?" I ask, not looking away from the me I missed so much.

Jeremy clears his throat, stepping into the room. "You passed out at Ratcliff's. We didn't know why, but we could tell you were still breathing."

Charlotte finishes. "We rushed you here and were looking up the hours for Birds of a Feather Chicken Rescue."

I turn to her. "Why?"

She shrugs. "There are no vets in town. We figured they could help."

God, what would these two do without me? Before I can point out that chickens and rats are very different, Jeremy continues the story, "Next thing, you were screaming for Charlotte, and I guess now you're back to being human."

I sit on the bed, resting my head in my hands. "I don't know how long this will last."

Charlotte sits next to me, running a hand down my bare back. I'm lost in my thoughts, but the simple friction pulls me out of myself, all my attention rushing toward her fingertips. I straighten, staring at her.

She notices the shift and her pupils dilate. "You're as handsome as I imagined you'd be."

I scrunch my face. "Not as much as him." I point to Jeremy, who joins me on the other side.

"I think the military fucked with your eyesight. You're clearly hot." He smirks.

My eyes widen. This must be a dream. Nobody has ever called me hot, let alone someone that looks like Jeremy.

Charlotte cups my chin and pulls my attention back to her. "How do you feel?"

I think about it for a second. "Fine. Not like I'm going to pop a tail anytime soon, at least."

"Why are you back to human?" Jeremy asks.

"I don't know. The scientists said I wasn't supposed to change back, but they also said I wasn't supposed to be conscious or able to talk, and clearly, they got that wrong. I guess they were wrong about this." My heart speeds, but I can't let the excitement overtake me. This could just be a fluke.

"Do you think it was the ratatouille?" Jeremy asks.

"What?" Charlotte and I both ask in unison.

"You ate a bite right before you passed out. Maybe that's the cure. Ratatouille takes away your ratness."

I shake my head and pat his cheek. "Jeremy, that's the fucking stupidest thing I've ever heard." I smile, and he rolls his eyes and pushes me away playfully.

There's no way to know why I'm back to my human form unless I want to return to Fort Pines and ask some questions, and that doesn't seem like the best idea. In fact, if I plan to stay here as a human, I'm going to need to come up with a disguise.

Charlotte grabs my chin, turning my attention to her. "We might never get answers to a lot of things. We don't even know if you'll stay a human."

"Wow,   " I deadpan. "How optimistic."

She grabs my shoulder, pulling me closer. "I'm just saying, this might be our only chance."

I know what she means—my bare cock pushes against the pillow—but I want to hear her say it. "Chance for what?"

She sighs. "To be together. All three of us."

I turn to Jeremy, already studying me with parted lips. "Is that what you both want? To fuck me as a man?" It's crass, but considering what I think we're about to do, it doesn't matter.

"Ramsay, I didn't want to fuck a rat. I wanted the you on the inside."

"I know, but now here I am—a man. Have you ever been with a man before?"

He shakes his head. "You're not just a man, you're you." Before I have time to argue, he pushes forward, grabbing my face and pulling my lips to his. It's my first kiss with a man—my first kiss in so fucking long, and it's almost too much. My hands find his neck, pulling him closer to me. I almost forget Charlotte's in the room with us, until the pillow is pulled off my lap, and her hands inch up my thighs. I separate from Jeremy's lips for just a second, regaining my composure. She settles to her knees on the floor before me, looking up at me with wide, awestruck eyes. I reach down, running my fingers through her silky, dark hair.

"Let me give you back the pleasure you gave me." She lowers her lips to the head of my cock, and my breath comes out as a wobbly plea. Jeremy grabs my chin, directing me to his lips again. "I don't know how long I'll last," I murmur against his lips.

"Shouldn't be a problem. You're a pro at coming more than once, after all." He smiles against me, and I bite his mouth. "No pressure," I respond.

Charlotte takes me deeper, her lips rolling and her tempo gentle. She comes up for a breath, a pop, and a string of saliva following. "God, you're big."

I grab her mouth. "I still bet you could take both of us at once." She moans against my hand, and I guide her back to my cock, sighing in pleasure once she makes contact.

I've witnessed Jeremy's cock from the top of his head. Everything seems larger when you're the size of a rat, but given the comparison of Charlotte's tight hole, I know it will be impressive. I reach for him, stroking his hardened length from the outside of his shorts. It's weird how much I want to feel him, lick him, take him until he's hitting the back of my throat. I've appreciated other men's forms before, gazed a little longer than I should in the barrack showers, but I've never wanted a dick more than I want Jeremy's. When I reach underneath his waistband and pull him free, my hand wrapping around him, my want reverberates deep in my bones.

He joked—or maybe he was being serious—that the ratatouille cured me of my ratness, but perhaps it could be that ridiculous. Life's ridiculous anyway. No, I don't think it was the stupid dish, but maybe my want for both of them was so great that I willed my cells to make the change.

I just play, running my fingers over his tip, feeling his bulging veins down his shaft. "I think we might be the same size," I whisper into his lips.

"I'll have to feel for myself."

His words—Charlotte's lips—it's too much. I jerk back, feeling my balls tighten, but she holds onto my legs, taking me deeper. I don't have time to stop, my cum shoots out of me violently. It's a lot, and I'm mortified that I didn't at least warn Charlotte. She doesn't seem to mind, though. She drinks me down eagerly, as if my cum is made of honey.

Jeremy whispers into my ear. "That's a good boy, come for us. So much cum in her tiny little mouth."

My consciousness returns to me, and I chuckle, rolling my forehead against Jeremy's. "When did you get so talkative?"

He shrugs. "I had a good teacher, after all."

Charlotte crawls up my legs, her lips puffy and even more fuckable. I pull her onto my lap and meet my lips to hers, tasting my salty flavor. I pull her thin dress up the expanse of her body, pulling it over her head. Her bare and wet cunt grinds against my leg. "No underwear? What a naughty girl," I say, taking a small break from her lips. Her small noises, the thought of my cum down her throat—all of it goes straight to my cock, raising my member to full mast.

"Look at that," Jeremy remarks. "I guess you're not all talk."

I look him in the eyes. "I want you to watch as I eat her pussy. This will be a lesson you won't want to miss." I flip her to her back, and her full breasts fall to the sides. God, I want to fuck every inch of her, but right now it's about her pleasure, about showing them both how good this can be for all of us. I kiss her lips gently, her breasts, her abdomen, and move even slower once I get to the apex of her thighs. I tease, kissing everywhere but her cunt. I lick her seam, and she squirms underneath me. Her hands run through my short hair, clawing at my scalp. "Please, Ramsay."

I sit up, looking Jeremy in the eye. He's removed his clothes—gloriously and deliciously naked. I almost lose myself at the sight, his defined muscles in every place they should be. I can see why he loves bodybuilding. His body is a piece of art and should be displayed. He intently watches us, stroking himself with his legs spread wide. I find my words. "See, you want her to beg like this. Don't let her come until she's squirming."

I dive back in, eagerly licking her from top to bottom. She cries out, grinding on my mouth. She wants me on her clit, I can tell in the way she arches her back, but I don't give in, not yet. I give her several more torturous strokes until I focus my attention on her sensitive bud. "Yes, just like that," she cries.

I pull away, and she sobs, but I need to make sure Jeremy is paying attention. His eyes are half-lidded, and his strokes are increasing in speed. "Good boy, Jeremy. I want you to come while you watch me. Don't take your eyes off her. She's going to look so pretty when she comes."

I apply direct pressure to her clit, moving my tongue ever so slightly. She erupts from underneath me, holding onto my shoulder to keep herself steady. I'm focused on Charlotte, wringing out every last drop of her pleasure, but I can't help but tune in as Jeremy cries out from next to us. I reach for him, grabbing his cock and lathering my hand in his pre cum at his tip. I push his hand away, stroking him until he releases. I rub his cum up and down his shaft until he's too sensitive to take any more.

I sit up from Charlotte's pussy, bending over to Jeremy's lips. "Taste her on me. She's so fucking good." I devour his lips, my hand not leaving his cock. "See. I told you. You're already so hard."

"Jesus fucking Christ," he mutters.

I pull back, grabbing Charlotte's slackened body and flipping her around so her ass is against my cock. She makes a little yelp but bucks her hips into me.

"Jeremy, choke her on your cock while I fuck her."

"Yes, sir."

My cock hardens even more that they're both taking my orders. They're my perfect little playthings, and I don't even have to pull hair to get them to do what I want.

Jeremy bends down, kissing Charlotte before she pulls away, desperate to have his dick in her mouth.

"God, girl. Take him just like that," I say, rubbing the tip of my cock against her sopping wet cunt.

Our eyes meet, and we both thrust into Charlotte. Her body vibrates with her moan. I've only managed to insert the tip, and she's barely taking more than that of Jeremy, but we both time our motions, thrusting into her at the perfect tempo.

Charlotte's small compared to us, so I lean forward and Jeremy meets me halfway. One of my hands grabs the back of his neck while the other rests in the hinge of Charlotte's hips, grounding myself as I pound into her. She's moaning around Jeremy's cock, but I know I could give her more. I reach around, sliding my fingers through her wet skin, circling her clit.

She cries out, and Jeremy thrusts deeper, causing her to gag. From the way she presses into me more, I can tell she loves it. She wants it harder and faster, and I'm anything if not her humble servant, ready to give her just what she deserves.

My muscles tense. I want us to come just like this—all three of us connecting. It's so fucking perfect, better than I could have ever imagined. I explore every inch of Jeremy's mouth, reveling in the feel of Charlotte's cunt constricting around me, focusing on the motions of my fingers as I strum her as if I'm wringing myself of the same pleasure she's feeling.

I've always searched for meaning—a purpose. I wanted to lose myself in a cause. The military took all of me, changing me into something I didn't even know anymore—literally. And yet, even with giving every part of myself, I never felt complete. Now, in this moment, connected to the two people I thought would never be mine, I feel whole. It's ridiculous. We're fucking. It's a crazy, porno fantasy brought to life, but it's everything to me. More than pleasure. More than a release. This is it.

As my second orgasm rolls through me and I feel and watch as Jeremy and Charlotte follow after me, mere seconds behind, I know it even more. We're made for each other—three imperfect pieces coming together to form a perfect binding.

I fall next to Charlotte on her bed, Jeremy doing the same on the other side of her. Part of me wonders if it will be awkward now, but we nuzzle into each other, sprinkling kisses over the nearest skin.

"God, I love you two." I don't even realize I say it. My body knows more than my brain will allow, and I tense, hoping the two will ignore it instead of explaining that it's too soon for such bold statements.

Charlotte turns to me, looking deep into my eyes. "I love you both, too." She rolls back to Jeremy. "I know it's soon, but that was too perfect to be anything but love."

Jeremy laughs. "Good, because I fucking love you both."

She kisses us, and Jeremy and I grab hands across Charlotte's body. I pull them as close as possible. Everything's perfect until the world starts to fade. I'm losing consciousness again, which could only mean one thing.

Chapter Sixteen

Charlotte

I 'm at my usual table, glancing at my watch, nervously tapping my foot. They've gotten so much better. Both of them took on this closing shift to save money for their upcoming competition. It's been fifteen minutes since I've seen either of them on the floor, which could only mean one thing.

Sure enough, Jeremy barrels out of the server station with a short white hat on his head. He rushes through the dining room, dropping drinks off, snagging empty plates, and leaving checks. He's moving full speed, making up for the lost time.

He's at the table nearest me, and I can hear whispers of his conversation with the green-skinned guest. "So sorry about the wait. Romeo has a health condition, and so I'll be helping him out for the rest of your dinner." The guest murmurs something back. "Oh, no, it's no trouble. He's actually my partner, so it's a pleasure to help him out." The guest nods praises. I click my tongue. She should leave a hefty tip after that spiel.

He turns away, heading toward me. Our eyes meet, and he shakes his head.

"It's been three days!" I exclaim.

"I know." He sighs. "Thankfully, it was when we were both in the server station alone." He picks his hat up, and Ramsay waves at me from underneath.

I wave, rolling my eyes. "Well, it's getting further apart. That's good."

Jeremy straightens his hat over his golden locks. "Yeah. I know."

"Well, be careful. Pay close attention to whether he passes out. You don't want a man appearing on your head." He leans down, kissing me on the cheek. "I'm always careful." He rushes away before I can argue because it's a blatant lie. That's one of the things I love about him. He's carefree, living on the edge, while Ramsay keeps us both in line. That's why we work so well together.

After Jeremy tends to his tables, he disappears again, not returning to the main floor for another ten minutes. When he emerges this time, Ramsay, or should I say, Romeo, follows after him. I breathe a sigh of relief. His time as a rat is getting shorter every shift. He wears thick-rimmed glasses and rubs at his full mustache above his lips—his new disguise while human. We all agreed that the authorities at Fort Pines aren't a massive threat to us, but we're close enough to the base that we should take caution while living in Ghostlight Falls. We love our quiet life here together too much to leave it behind.

The two men work together, clearing out their last two tables. Romeo's attention snags on me, and his usual focused expression shifts, warming up into a rosy smile. He jogs over to me, leaning down to kiss me on the lips. "Miss me?"

"You're never really gone."

"Yeah, but I'm a much better server when I'm in my man body."

"And much sexier." I pull him by his collar to my lips again.

He pulls away. "Okay, save that for later. Let us close this place down." He jogs ahead, Jeremy following behind and subtly smacking him on the ass.

I turn back to witness the green-skinned guest at the table next to me, the one Jeremy had spoken to earlier, giving me a scrunched- face look. I stick my tongue out at her. It's surprising, usually her species of alien isn't so judgy, but I guess every walk of life has its own type of Karen.

I ignore her, eating the last bites of my ratatouille. I've tried other dishes at Ratcliff's, but this one is still my favorite. I think it's senti-mental to me now.

The woman next to me signs her check and slides out of her seat, scoffing as she walks by me toward the exit. I'm the last guest in the restaurant. It's usually like this on the nights my boys close. I watch as Jeremy and Ramsay wipe off the last table, laughing with each other as they clock out and take off their aprons. I can never get enough of them. Sometimes I wish I could change into a tiny rodent and spend my time observing, completely unnoticed. Their love is so palpable, and I still pinch myself that it's something I get to be a part of. All my life, I felt lonely. Now I feel seen and wanted at all moments.

They share a quick kiss before meeting me at the table. "You ready?" Jeremy asks as he extends a hand to pull me to my feet. I accept his offering, and he crashes his lips against mine. Ramsay works on clearing my table quickly. He runs my empty plates back to the kitchen and scurries back to us. I greet him, kissing him on his scratchy lips. "I owe you a tip."

He smirks, kissing down my neck. "How about you repay me once we get home?"

My cheeks heat with the anticipation of what's in store. "I can do that." I grab his hand and turn toward the exit.

Jeremy grabs my other hand. "Hey, don't I get a tip? I refilled your drink earlier tonight."

I kiss his cheek. "Of course you do." I grab his hand. "But you two are suckers, because it's really all just a treat for me."

My two men lean in, kissing me before we walk. We leave Ratcliff's behind us, the quiet city of Ghostlight Falls greeting us as we step into the cool night air. It won't be long before the three of us are home, and then I'll be romanced by my two charming men—one of them that still sometimes turns into a rat, but who's never anything less than a man to me.

Chapter Seventeen

Jeremy

I'm so goddamn full. Last time I was sure Ramsay's giant cock would split me in two, but this time is perfect, better than perfect, out of this fucking world. Of course, when he slowly inserted himself, the pressure was tremendous, but now that he's sunk completely into me and my cock is buried into Charlotte's cunt, no pain exists in my body. In fact, I can't even remember what pain feels like anymore. All I am is a vessel of liquid pleasure, and my brain is sludge. It's normal, though. I never have to think too hard when I'm with Ramsay.

"That's a good boy. Taking my cock so good. You like it, don't you? Love it when I'm fucking you both."

"Yes!" I cry, sinking my teeth into Charlotte's shoulder to steady myself.

Ramsay continues his shallow thrusts and I match his speed as Charlotte grips around my cock. We're going slow. We must if we want this to last longer than thirty seconds. It's been six months together—fucking like animals every chance we get—but it never gets old to us. It only gets better and better.

Ramsay runs his fingers through my hair, tugging slightly.

"Don't do that. I'll come if you pull," I yell desperately.

Ramsay tsks, still playing with my locks as he fucks me. "Already? I thought you were the man who only came once. This would be your third time in the last hour." He'll never let me live down that misconception of myself.

"It's up to you," I say through labored breaths.

"That's right. Good boy. I'll tell you both when you're allowed to come again." His smooth tail slides against my thigh, moving upwards and around my body to Charlotte underneath me as she holds herself up on all fours. Her pussy clamps around me and I cry out. Ramsay must have used his rat tail to play with her clit.

It's been two months since Ramsay transformed back into a rat. We think he's completely back in his human form now, even though he's not entirely the same. He's able to keep his new human-sized rat tail hidden during his shifts at Ratcliff's and out and about in town. No one would bat an eye at his extra appendage—this is Ghostlight Falls, after all—but we're still wary of the government putting the pieces together.

I'm thankful I can love Ramsay as a man all the time now, but the tail is a nice addition, especially in the bedroom.

"Ramsay, it's too much." She cries, and I can feel in the way her body tenses that she's telling the truth.

Ramsay reaches under me, caressing her jaw. "You can go a little longer, sweetheart. I know it." He pounds into me, nearly knocking me off balance, and smushing Charlotte underneath me. If it weren't for his intense training, making me the most built I've ever been in my life for my upcoming competition, I wouldn't have been able to keep myself up. He's as big, if not bigger than me. He loves to push me toward my edge, both in the gym and in the bedroom. It's why I can't get enough of him.

As his speed increases inside of me, so does the euphoria. From all ends, I'm filled and filling. I breathe in Charlotte's almond shampoo, kissing the back of her neck as I caress her breast.

"I'm so close!" she cries.

Her sweet words, Ramsay's cock, the way his hands grip my hips as he thrusts inside of me—I'm right there with her.

Ramsay knows us so well. He grabs my hair, pulling the strand that forces hot semen to shoot out of me and into Charlotte. Ramsay comes at the same time. I thought I had no room left inside of me, but his cum fills me even more, adding to the sensation and dripping down my ass. Charlotte follows right after us. I feel so lucky that I'm the one who gets to feel the grip of her orgasm this time. She milks me for every last drop, her body relaxing as her breath returns to a regular tempo.

Ramsay runs a hand down my back as he pulls out of me. I immediately miss the sensation. I probably could go for a fourth time if the other two were up to it. But as I lift all my weight off Charlotte and she drops to the bed, Ramsay collapsing next to her, I realize my partners might need a second to recover. I follow after them, cradling Charlotte from behind. She nestles back into me as Ramsay peppers kisses down her face. "You were so good. You took us both perfectly."

Ramsay reaches over and grabs my hand, bringing it to his lips. "How was that for you? Was it enough lube?" His tail snakes over and runs up and down my thigh.

"So fucking good." My lungs are still working to return to their normal rhythm.

He kisses my hand again.

We lie there for a moment longer. The only sounds are our soft kisses and happy little grunts as we cozy into each other. The moment is so perfect, but all my moments are when I'm with these two. Sometimes

I worry they'll grow tired of hearing how much I love them, but they tell me they never will.

I still can't believe this is my life, and all because I decided to trust a rat to take the reins.

Thanks for Reading

Thank you for reading! If you enjoyed *Romanced by the Rat*, please make sure to leave a review.

Want more of G.M. Fairy? Check out her other books...

Pounded by Produce: A Veggie Love Tale

A tale of veggies tempted to break their vows.

Fleeing a tumultuous past, Emily finds refuge at a kitchen job in a quiet countryside parish.

Robert and Laurent are two best friends with a bond that has crossed lines throughout their history but now walk the straight and narrow, giving their lives to their parish as priests

One magical night under the harvest moon, Robert and Laurent experience a bizarre transformation: They wake up as a tomato and cucumber.

Emily brings these ripe and juicy vegetables into the kitchen, but instead of preparing a meal, she uses them for other, more carnal needs. Emily awakens something inside of the priests, who switch back and forth between their human and vegetable forms.

The three find themself in a steamy entanglement, unable to deny their primal desires. Will they fight their urges or break their vows and alter the course of their lives forever?

Get In My Swamp: The Completed Series

The three-part best-selling and viral sensation *Get In My Swamp* is now in one place.

Book 1 *Get In My Swamp*: When Liona stumbles upon Beck, the ogre's trap, and becomes his prisoner, she's determined to escape. But it doesn't take long for things to start heating up between the two. Beck is trying to protect her, and Liona can't help her body's reaction to the buff green monster. The lines between captive and captor become blurry, and the passion becomes a raging fire neither of them can put out.

Book 2 *Stay In My Swamp*: Life in the swamp can't get any better for Liona and Beck. That's until Beck pops a big question that forces Liona to face some unfinished business. She heads back to LA but Beck isn't too far behind, this time looking less like an ogre thanks to some help from Winston the Wizard. Will magic be enough for Beck to get Liona to stay in his swamp forever?

Book 3 and Standalone *Spellbound Seduction*: Winston the Wizard is a master of magic but a stranger to love. He has a full life in the hidden world of the magical community, but lives with a condition that makes it impossible to fully connect. He's content with his life as the manager of Happily Ever Endings, a club for adult enchantments, until he meets Marigold- a young woman who suffers from a similar condition, and she needs his help to take her on a journey to cure her curse. Winston feels an instant connection to her but knows they can never be. Can he resist temptation to keep them both alive? Or will he succumb to his urges and ruin them both?

Stay up to date on all things G.M. Fairy!

Check out all the stories in the Ghostlight Falls series!

Mappy McMapface
Nicole Parker

Paper and Passion
Thea Masen

Bread by the Grim
Dakota Cockaday

Demons and Dustjackets
Sabrina Cross

Luna Cantrip
Twi-flight

Taking a Tumble
Clover Holloway

Defined and Defiled
Elsie LePlant

Cirrus About You
Latrexa Nova

Hello, Nurse!
Nicole Parker

Her Wonderful Wonder Belle
Sylvia Morrow

Knot Falling In Love
Kenzie James